Fear My Gangsta 5

D1452504

Tranay Adams

Lock Down Publications and Ca$h
Presents
Fear My Gangsta 5
A Novel by *Tranay Adams*

Fear My Gangsta 5

Lock Down Publications
P.O. Box 944
Stockbridge, Ga 30281

Visit our website @
www.lockdownpublications.com

Copyright by Tranay Adams
Fear My Gangsta 5

Lock Down Publications
Like our page on Facebook: Lock Down Publications @
www.facebook.com/lockdownpublications.ldp
Cover design and layout by: **Dynasty Cover Me**
Book interior design by: **Shawn Walker**
Edited by: **Lashonda Johnson**

Tranay Adams

Stay Connected with Us!

Text **LOCKDOWN** to 22828 to stay up-to-date with new releases, sneak peaks, contests and more...

Thank you!

Submission Guideline.

Submit the first three chapters of your completed manuscript to ldpsubmissions@gmail.com, subject line: Your book's title. The manuscript must be in a .doc file and sent as an attachment. Document should be in Times New Roman, double spaced and in size 12 font. Also, provide your synopsis and full contact information. If sending multiple submissions, they must each be in a separate email.

Have a story but no way to send it electronically? You can still submit to LDP/Ca$h Presents. Send in the first three chapters, written or typed, of your completed manuscript to:

LDP: Submissions Dept
P.O. Box 944
Stockbridge, Ga 30281

DO NOT send original manuscript. Must be a duplicate.

Provide your synopsis and a cover letter containing your full contact information.

Thanks for considering LDP and Ca$h Presents.

Tranay Adams

Chapter One

Ezra spent six hours in Fear's closet waiting for him to come back home. He'd lost track of time and found himself dozing off a few times. Figuring his mark wasn't returning home that night, Ezra decided to see if he could catch him at the hospital. If he didn't find him there, Gustavo gave him strict orders to take care of his fiancée. He reasoned that if he couldn't get to Fear, he was going to take the lives of everyone he loves. Gustavo was one cold-hearted mothafucka!

Ezra was disguised as a blue-eyed, big nose, Caucasian doctor when he walked inside the hospital. As he strolled through the first-floor lobby, he glanced at the wall to wall mirror, taking in his reflection. He smiled seeing his long blonde hair was pulled back into a ponytail, his blue scrubs, and his lab coat, with his work badge clipped to it.

Not too bad considering this is my first-time dressing in a disguise for a hit. I don't even recognize myself. This shit is kinda creeping me out.

Ezra made his way through the metal detector. It didn't go off which was normal since he wasn't packing his blower. He made his way over to the security guard sitting behind the desk, playing a game on his cell phone. He asked him what floor Italia White was on. The security guard looked at his chart and told him. Ezra thanked him, went about his business, and hopped on the elevator. He made his way onto the sixth floor. Emerging from the elevator, he made a right and walked down the hallway. Then, he made a left and continued down the corridor. Ezra whistled as he pulled on a pair of black leather gloves, flexing his fingers inside of them. Once he was inside of Italia's room, which was dark besides a dim light shining on her face, he watched her from the shadows.

Senorita, you're so bello, it's a shame you have to morir, I'd much rather matar your man, Ezra thought. *I guess you'll do—for now.*

Only the lower half of Ezra was seen as he pulled out a small bottle of poison and a syringe. He slid the needle of the syringe through the top of the bottle and withdrew some of its contents.

Next, he put the bottle inside his pocket and smiled wickedly, as he approached Italia's bedside. He removed the IV from her arm, which left her shunt visible. Carefully, he slid the syringe inside the shunt and prepared to apply pressure to its plunger.

"Good night, Sleeping Beauty—forever. Aaaahhh!" Ezra threw his head back screaming in agony, as a black nightstick slammed down against his arm. He released the syringe and staggered backward.

The nightstick swung through the air and cracked him in his jaw. The impact dislodged a tooth and bloodied his mouth. Then the nightstick slammed into his stomach and he doubled over, howling in pain. His assailant slipped behind him and pulled his nightstick against his neck, choking him. Ezra's eyes bulged and he gritted, veins engorged in his forehead. He slipped his fingers underneath the nightstick trying to lighten the pressure against his throat, but his efforts were to no avail. His assailant was much stronger.

Ezra and his assailant struggled for power over the nightstick. They clenched their teeth and flexed the muscles in their jaws. Veins bulged on their foreheads and their faces shone from perspiration. Suddenly, the assailant swiftly jerked his nightstick to the left and violently snapped Ezra's neck, killing him. The assailant, Lester released Ezra from the hold of the nightstick and allowed his lifeless body to collapse to the floor. Looking down at his handiwork, Lester breathed heavily and wiped his sweaty forehead with the back of his hand.

"Young, punk mothafucka," Lester said as he sheathed his nightstick at his side.

He locked Italia's room door, grabbed Ezra by his ankles, and dragged him into the bathroom. He stripped him naked and placed him inside the shower. He brought his duffle bag inside the bathroom and unzipped it. Quickly, he got dressed in a shower-cap, surgical mask, smock, latex gloves, and shoe coverings. He pulled out his cell phone and placed it up on the sink, setting it to play a song by Frank Sinatra. Lester went about the task of draining Ezra's body of its blood, chopping up his body with the bladed tools from his bag, and storing the pieces into two separate black heavy-duty garbage bags.

Once he tied the bags up, he set them aside and scrubbed and wiped the shower clean. Next, he pulled out two long aluminum spray cans and sprayed the floor and walls of the shower. After storing the spray cans and the blades back inside the bag, he took out a ten-inch stick. He smacked the stick against his knee, and it turned on, shining brightly. When he cut off the bathroom light, the stick was glowing neon blue. The stick became a UV light.

Lester swept the stick over the shower's ceiling, walls, and floor. He couldn't find a trace of blood, which was how he wanted it. He smacked the stick against his knee again and killed its light. He then cut on the bathroom's light, stored the glow stick inside his bag, and pulled off the protective coverings. Once he made sure there weren't any stains of blood on him, Lester stashed his bag inside the closet in Italia's room and grabbed the two garbage bags containing Ezra's severed body parts. Once he made sure the coast was clear, he snuck down to the trash shoot and dumped the garbage bags inside of it. He walked off smacking the imaginary dust from his hands and whistling. Returning to Italia's bathroom, he approached her bedside and studied her face for a while.

"Seeing how A.J. is going through all of this trouble for you. You must be a very special young lady to him," Lester told Italia.

Fear had hollered at him so he could watch her back for him. At first, he wasn't tripping off having someone up there with Italia around the clock, but he had this nagging feeling that he should send someone up there to hold her down. Once he'd gotten the news about what had gone down in his absence. Lester was sure Fear was going to be extremely grateful for making the decision to send him to the hospital.

***

Las Vegas

Fear sat low inside the limousine tinted, 2013 Dodge Challenger SRT8 he'd stolen out of the Barbary Coast gentlemen's club parking lot. He'd spent the past six hours staking out the Palms Casino Resort, where he saw two big, Russian, white men enter with a band of women. All the women were fine as hell and dressed sexily. Fear watched the ladies, or whores as they were called by the white men as they walked toward the house in a single file line. The way the Russians were overseeing them made them look like African slaves heading into the field to pick cotton.

Now, to the untrained eye, it would appear as if the Russians were just chaperones for a few exotic dancers. Fear could tell by the way the white men were walking that they were strapped. They not only had guns on them, but they had walking canes that doubled as cattle-prods. So, if any of the women got out of line they'd zap their ass to put them back in their place. Fear witnessed this when one of the girls didn't get out of the van fast enough for the Russians. He wanted to hop out and beat his ass, but he didn't want to ruin his element of surprise. Besides, he was being paid specifically to apprehend Drake's daughter, Ariel and that's exactly what he was going to do.

Fear knew the Russian men were going to give him the most trouble. So, he'd have to make short work of them if he was going to rescue Ariel. As far as he could tell there weren't any more hands he'd have to worry about besides the Russians. He didn't see anyone following their van, acting as security for them. He reasoned they must have been acting as their own security and guarding the women as well. This was perfect for Fear. He knew exactly how he was going to follow through with his assignment now. He hoped things didn't get bloody, but if they did, he was well prepared for it.

Fear sat up when he saw the Russians and the ladies leaving the hotel. He pulled a White Sox baseball cap over his brows and tied a bandana over the lower half of his face. He fired up his car. As soon as the van carrying the girls pulled off, he did too, following right behind it. He made sure to keep a safe distance from them. He didn't want them getting suspicious. Keeping an eye on the streets, Fear opened the glove box and removed a Ghost gun.

Once they stopped at a red traffic light, he screwed a silencer on the barrel of it and cocked it. He tucked the gun back inside his jacket and pulled off after the van when the traffic light turned green. Fear allowed the van to get a nice distance from him before he sped after it. He rammed it from behind, violently. The driver lost control of the van, it swung around and flipped over several times. It landed hard on its side and slid into the intersection, blocking traffic. Smoke began to rise from its busted radiator.

The horrified drivers of other vehicles looked on and hoped everyone aboard was okay. Some of them got out of their cars to check on the van's passengers. That was until Fear flew like a bat out of hell from down the street and swung his Dodge Challenger around. The car skirted to a stop, diagonally. The driver's door open and he hopped out, toting a tool used to snatch out entire locks. He stuck the tool inside of his belt. Using the van's side-view mirror, he climbed up on it and used his tool to snatch out the lock. Everyone watched as he did this while filming him on their cell phones. He didn't give a rat's ass. He was focused on the mission at hand and he was going to carry it out.

After Fear snatched the lockout, he stuck the tool inside his belt and opened the door of the van. The women inside cried out in pain. Some of them had bruises on their faces and were bleeding at the corner of their foreheads. Fear started helping them out of the wrecked van one by one. He searched frantically for Ariel as he did so.

"Ariel! Ariel!" Fear called out over and over again.

"Yeah?" A pretty, brown-skinned girl looked up at Fear.

Instantly, he recognized her as the young woman from the picture. She looked a lot like her father, Drake, and even had a British accent like him.

"Your father sent me to rescue you. Come with me. I'll make sure you get back to 'em." Fear extended his hand.

Ariel looked at his hand hesitantly because she wasn't sure if he was trying to trick her or not. Throwing caution to the wind, she grasped his hand and he pulled her up on the van. He was helping her down the side of the van when he heard someone calling out to him. He looked back over into the doorway of the van and saw a slim-thick, cinnamon complexioned woman. She had shoulder-length locs, hazel brown eyes, and full succulent lips. She had a real exotic look to her. In fact, with her features, little mama could have been a superstar runway model. Unfortunately, she became a victim of sex trafficking so that was out of the question.

"Help me! Help me, please!" The exotic looking woman called out to Fear.

She was reaching out to him. He pulled her up on the outside of the van and jumped down to the ground. He then held his hands up to her. He told her to jump down into his arms. She reluctantly did so, he caught her and placed her down gently on the asphalt. She stared into his eyes for a moment and became lost in them. He had just saved her life, so he was like her knight in shining armor. She felt like she owed him. So, right then, she vowed to repay him in whichever way she could.

"Are you okay?" Fear asked her as he held her by the waist. A concerned look was in his eyes. She nodded yes. "Look, you should get outta here. The cops are coming!" he pulled out the Ghost gun, grabbed Ariel by her hand, and took off running toward his Dodge Challenger.

Unbeknownst to them, one of the Russians had kicked out the broken windshield of the van. He posted up with his back against the grill of it and held his gun up to his shoulder. There was a nasty, bloody gash above his left brow, but he wasn't paying it any mind. He was solely focused on blowing out the brains of the fuck that caused the accident. While this was going on, all the women Fear had helped out of the van had scattered all over the streets.

They were running back and forth across Fear's line of vision as he made his way toward his stolen whip. Once the last of the women had cleared out of his path, the Russian jumped out from in front of the van and pointed his gun at him. But before he could pull the trigger, Fear sent some hot shit at him and his brains flew out the back of his skull. The Russian fell into the street. His eyes and mouth were wide open. Horror was written across his face.

"Come on!" Fear pulled Ariel along, but she had problems keeping up.

She realized it was her high heel pumps that were slowing her down. So, she made him stop so she could take them off. She took the pumps in her hand and ran off with Fear. Feeling a presence above her, she looked up and saw the last Russian in midair. He'd leaped off the top of the van and landed on Fear. They impacted the street and the Ghost gun slid ten feet away from them.

The Russian turned Fear over on his back and started punching him in the face. The barbaric nature of his attack left the assassin barely conscious. His eyes were rolled to the back of his head and he was groaning in pain. Pulling out his gun, the Russian cocked it and stuck it into Fear's mouth.

The Russian hatefully stared down at Fear and said, "Potseluy svoyu chernuyu zadnitsu do svidaniya!" Kiss your black ass goodbye!

The Russian threw his head back hollering as a sharp pain exploded in his shoulder, causing him to drop his gun. He became enraged. His face turned red and veins bulged on his forehead. He whipped around to his assailant and found Ariel. Spooked, she slowly walked backward from him. He pulled the high heel pump out she'd stabbed him in his shoulder with, looked at it, and threw it aside. He clenched his jaws angrily. He then stood upright and stalked after Ariel.

She turned to run but he grabbed her by her hair and pulled her into him. She hollered out in pain as she felt fire rip through her scalp. The Russian whipped her around, so she'd be facing him. When she looked into his eyes, she could see the evil in them. An icy chill slid down her back and her heart thudded madly. She was scared and didn't know what to do. This mothafucka was huge. He was four times her size. Hell, on top of that he was as strong as an ox.

"I'm gonna squeeze your pretty little neck 'til your head pops like a zit!" the crazed Russian swore.

He clasped his big, strong, vein riddle hands around Ariel's neck and lifted her off her feet. Ariel gagged and coughed feeling the five pounds of pressure against her windpipe cutting off the oxygen that passed through her lungs. Her face turned red and the veins at her temples throbbed, blood clots formed in the whites of her eyes, and her eyes turned glassy. She was on the verge of tears. She swung her legs back and forth. She was trying desperately to get out of the Russian's clutches, but she wasn't any match for his brute strength. Tears rolled down Ariel's cheeks and her eyelids fluttered. She found herself growing light-headed.

Her vision became blurry and began to fade. Her grip loosened on the Russian's wrists and the swinging of her legs slowed. When the Russian saw Ariel on the tight rope of death it seemed to excite him. Madness danced in his pupils and a wicked smile spread across his face.

"Oh, yeah, bitch. When you get to hell—give Satan a kiss for me." The Russian kissed Ariel on her open mouth tenderly.

When he pulled his head back from her, his eyes exploded open and his jaw dropped. He released Ariel from his grasp, and she crashed to the street. She lay where she was gagging, coughing, and rubbing her neck. She tried desperately to catch her breath as her vision slowly came back into focus.

The Russian turned around wearing a shocked expression on his face. He found the exotic looking woman at his back. She was clutching Fear's gun as it expelled smoke into the night's cool air. The young lady's eyes were glassy and frightening. She'd wanted to put something hot through that baldhead-fuck for as long as she could remember. The Russian threw his head back and screamed out in frustration. He looked back at the exotic woman and charged at her.

Little mama didn't even flinch. She wasn't afraid at all. In fact, she stood her ground with her gun trained on him. She squeezed off three shots, all of which struck him in his upper chest. The bullets didn't slow his big ass down. He was still coming at her. Full speed ahead! She reasoned it was because he was enraged, and his adrenaline was pumping one-hundred miles an hour. Homeboy didn't show any signs of slowing down.

The Russian was quickly closing the distance between him and the exotic woman. Still, she didn't show any signs of fear. Fear lay on the ground, he licked his bloody lip. His head snapped back and forth between the Russian and the exotic woman. A frown manifested on his face. He didn't know what the fuck old girl was waiting for, but she should have been popped his ass.

"Slim, what the fuck are you waiting on? Knock this nigga's head off!" Fear called out to her.

The exotic woman didn't move a muscle. She was totally focused on the Russian. She took a deep breath and relaxed. She squeezed her left-eye shut and took aim at the charging brute. She lined the sighting on the gun up with the area she wanted the bullet to land. Next, she gently placed her finger on the trigger. The Russian was ready to pounce on her. His feet were about to leave the pavement when the exotic woman pulled the trigger. The handgun slightly jerked within her grasp. An empty, smoking, shell-casing hopped out of the gun as it released a silver bullet. The bullet appeared to be moving fast, but slow at the same time to the exotic woman.

A nickel-sized hole appeared on the Russian's forehead and the back of his head exploded. Blood, pieces of skull, and brain fragments went flying everywhere. The big man, with terror on his face, collapsed to the street, dead. The exotic woman lowered the gun and took another breath. She watched as Fear grabbed Ariel's hand and took off running toward her.

While in motion, he grabbed her hand and continued booking toward his Dodge Challenger. Quickly, they all jumped inside the stolen car and slammed their respective doors shut. Fear fired up the whip and peeled out, leaving smoke behind in his wake.

Fear had gotten several blocks ahead by the time the police arrived, and a police helicopter was sweeping the area from above. He glanced back and forth over his shoulder as he whipped up the street. He blew past pedestrians, other vehicles, houses, and businesses in the hood. He didn't bother slowing down to normal speed until he was clear of the hot zone.

"Is everyone okay?" Fear looked between the exotic woman

and Ariel. They both nodded yes. "Good. Ariel, I'ma drop you off to your pops. And you, what's your name?" he looked to the exotic woman and waited for her to report her name.

"Constance," the exotic woman told him.

"Nice to meet chu, Constance. You can call me Fear." Fear then extended his hand over his shoulder and introduced himself to Ariel.

"Look, you've gotta take us somewhere to remove these tracking devices," Constance told him.

She turned on the dome light in the ceiling. She gripped her locs into a ponytail and turned her head, pointing to an area behind her ear. Fear narrowed his eyelids and took a quick glance. He saw a small healed scar laying over a lump the size of a small shirt-button. "You see it? It's right there."

"Yeah, I see it," he assured her.

"I've got one, too. In fact, all the girls under Momma had one surgically implanted on them. This way she'll be able to find us wherever we are in the world," Ariel informed him. "You've gotta get somewhere and remove them quick. She probably already sent The Hunters to fetch us by now. We're already outside of the coverage zone."

Anytime Momma got a call for the girls for work, she programmed the tracking devices in them to only span so far before they started beeping like crazy. When they did, she'd know that the girls were trying to flee from their life of captivity. So, if the chaperones didn't call to inform her that they'd made a quick stop somewhere outside of the coverage area. She wouldn't waste any time sending the Hunter Killaz out to recover them. Once the girls were brought back home, they'd get either sodomized, beaten, or have their clits cut off so they'd never feel pleasure again. Shit, sometimes Momma's Hunters were given orders to track the runaway girls down and execute them on sight. It all depended on how valuable they were to her business.

"Okay. There's a 76-Gas station coming up ahead." Fear nodded to the gas station coming up on his right side. The girls looked to confirm it. "I've got my blade on me. I can remove them inside the bathroom."

Tranay Adams

Chapter Two

Momma stepped out of the tub and snatched her towel off the rack, drying off. She wrapped the towel around her and sauntered into her bedroom. She grabbed a bottle of lotion and sat down on the bed, proceeding to rub some up and down her legs at a time. Hearing her cellular ring on the nightstand, she glanced at its screen. Seeing who it was, she picked it up and adjusted her Bluetooth on her ear, answering the call.

"Yes?" Momma asked as she continued to lotion up her legs and arms. When she heard the news of the girls escaping from the crash and her Russian chaperones being killed, she stopped putting lotion on.

"What the fuck? Those bitches! Gemme a second!" She pulled open the top drawer of her nightstand and took out a device the size of a Kindle Fire reader.

She operated it through its touchscreen, opening a window that showed two red dots with names beside them, moving through a mapped layout of Las Vegas.

"Look, stay on 'em no matter what. If they're running, then they've probably removed the tracking devices." Momma disconnected the call and opened a smaller window in the corner of the map, which gave an option to detonate. She tapped the detonate option.

***

Fear, Ariel, and the exotic woman ran out of the 76-Gas station restroom. Fear was still holding a hunting knife with a bloody tip in his hand. He'd just removed the tracking devices from behind the girl's ear that doubled as an explosive. As they were hauling ass back to Fear's whip, they spotted two black leather-clad motorcyclists zipping up the block and looking in their direction.

Ka-boom!

The restroom suddenly exploded, and everyone dove to the

ground, narrowly missing the restroom's door flying toward their heads. Fire and smoke rushed out of the restroom's doorway. When one of the motorcyclists saw the explosion, he motioned for the other motorcyclist to follow him and they sped toward the gas station. Fear saw the motorcyclists speeding in their direction. He grasped Ariel's hand, and she, in turn, grasped Constance's hand. Together, they dashed to his whip and jumped in. Fear fired up the stolen Dodge and sped out of the gas station lot. Looking up in the rearview mirror, he saw the motorcyclists heading for them.

"Oh, shit! They're coming for us! They're fucking coming for us!" Ariel said in a panic, looking through the back window and seeing the motorcyclists.

"Who the fuck are *they*?" Fear asked, looking back and forth between the windshield and Constance. She was in the front passenger seat, looking in the side-view mirror at the motorcyclists, too.

"Hunter Killaz!" Constance answered, her eyes glued to the side-view mirror.

"What the fuck are Hunter Killaz?" Fear's forehead creased, wondering.

"They work for Momma," Constance answered, watching the Hunter Killaz get closer and closer. "They're like the fucking slave catchers of the twenty-first century. Their job is to catch us and bring us back—dead or alive," when she said this, she looked Fear right in his eyes. The look in her eyes told him that she was dead serious.

Drake is really making me work for my coins tonight, isn't he? Fear thought of the businessman that had hired him to rescue his daughter, Ariel.

He popped open the glove box and removed a Tech-9, passing it to Constance. He smacked the glove box shut and watched her with the semi-automatic. Lil' mama was examining it like she was trying to figure out how to use it.

"Look, cock the slide on it, point it at the mothafuckaz that's tryna kill us, and pull the trigger. Simple enough, right?" Fear looked at Constance and she nodded.

She checked the magazine of the Tech-9 and made sure it was fully loaded. Once she smacked it back into the semi-automatic, she cocked it, and hung halfway out of the passenger window. The air rushed against Constance, ruffling her locs and dress. She held the Tech-9 firmly in her hands and aimed it at the motorcyclist closest to her. At the same time, he was lifting his Mac-10, but she already had the drop on him. Constance pulled the trigger of the Tech-9 and it vibrated in her hands, spitting fire. Bullets zipped up the motorcyclist's torso, chest, and shattered the sun-visor of his helmet. The motorcyclist went limp on his Ducati Supersport and it went off course to his right.

Craaaashhh!

The dead motorcyclist's Ducati slammed into the back of a parked Yukon Denali. The impact lifted him off his bike, making him do a back flip in the air, landing flat on his back.

"He's coming, he's coming!" Ariel screamed from the back seat.

The second motorcyclist had drawn his Mac-10 and was speeding alongside the Dodge. Constance tried to draw a bead on him with her Tech-9, but he'd gotten out of her sight. The motorcyclist was quickly moving up alongside the Dodge. He had planned to murder Fear which would immobilize his vehicle, leaving the female passengers at his mercy. Fear saw the motorcyclist on the side of him, pointing his Mac-10 right at him. He grabbed the motorcyclist's wrist and pointed his semi-automatic in a different direction, as it fired rapidly.

"Oh, you done fucked up! You done really fucked up now!" Fear scowled, looking back and forth between the motorcyclist and the windshield. He was holding the motorcyclist's wrist with one hand and steering the car with the other. Constance was trying to get a shot at the motorcyclist, but Fear was in the way.

Meanwhile, Ariel was lying on the backseat screaming her fucking head off. She really wasn't used to this gangsta ass shit!

"You fucked with the wrong one, nigga! The wrong fucking one!" Fear mashed the gas pedal to the floor, speeding up the Dodge. He was going so fast that the cars parked on either side of him turned into blurs.

Ba-boom!

The motorcyclist slammed into the side-view mirror of a parked Ford Explorer. The impact knocked him off his Ducati Supersport and sent it tumbling down the street. Fear looked at the side view mirror and saw the motorcyclist tumbling out into the intersection, stopping. The motorcyclist who was obviously in pain, slowing started to get up. Speeding motorists whipped back and forth across the motorcyclist, narrowly missing him, and madly honking their horns. When the motorcyclist looked up, he saw a big ass Mac truck coming at him full speed ahead. He screamed and threw up his arms. The next minute the Mac truck ran him over, crushing him. First, there were the front wheels, then the middle wheels, and finally the back wheels. The Mac truck screeched to a stop! The only thing left in the intersection of the motorcyclist was a pile of bloody, mutilated flesh.

Fear was looking at the tragic ending of the motorcyclist the entire time through the side-view mirror. He threw his head back laughing maniacally at his expense. He looked at Constance and Ariel and they were laughing as well. They all smacked each other high-fives.

***

"Shiiittt!" Momma threw her device in a fit of rage and it ricocheted off the wall. The device allowed her to see everything from the Hunter Killaz' point of view. She'd just witnessed the last one being run over by an eighteen-wheeler.

***

On the ride back to Los Angeles, Fear stopped by 7-11 to pick up some peroxide, A & D ointment, and needle and thread. He cleaned the wounds behind Ariel and Constance's ears, applied the ointment to it and stitched it up. Four hours later, Fear was pulling inside the parking lot of Burger King, located in the city of

Hawthorne on El Segundo Blvd. This was where he was supposed to link up with Ariel's father, Drake.

"Fuck is yo pops, Ariel? Nigga was 'pose to have been here." Fear glanced at his digital timepiece.

At that exact moment, a sleek, black Mercedes-Benz sprinter van pulled up beside Fear's Dodge Challenger and the side door of it opened. A white nigga in a fitted black suit hopped out wearing an earpiece. If Fear didn't know any better, he would have sworn that homeboy was One Time. But he knew Hahn didn't fuck with anyone who dealt with the police. That meant that old boy had to be a part of Drake's professional security team who had a license to kill. Fear believed this wholeheartedly because Drake wasn't involved in the streets. He had his hands in legitimate businesses. That's how he made his bread. He only had Hahn's contact for situations like this. You know when a nigga couldn't call the police. He had to hit up some certified killaz who didn't mind dropping a body or two to get shit done.

Once the security guard stepped out, he stood at the rear of the van and kept a close eye on things. The other security riding in the van hopped out. He went to stand at the grill of the van to keep his eyes on things. If any drama popped off, they'd lay down their lives to protect their boss and his daughter. They were being paid a small fortune to do so, so they didn't mind.

Drake was the last one to step out of the van. He was all smiles when he laid his eyes on his daughter. He opened his arms to her as she hopped out of the car and ran around it with her arms opened. She and her father embraced. Her body shook as she cried her eyes out. Tears accumulated in Drake's eyes and threatened to fall too, but he blinked them back. No matter how touching the moment was, he preferred to show strength at all times. That was just the type of man he'd always been.

"Oh, daddy, I thought I'd never see you again. I love you so much!" Ariel swore as tears continued to slide down her cheeks. Green snot threatened to drip from her left-nostril, but she snorted it back up her nose.

"I love you, too, baby girl. You ready to go home?" Drake

asked her as he held her at arm's length. She nodded yes.

They held one another for a while longer before they broke their embrace. Ariel ran over to the driver's side of Fear's Dodge Challenger. She thanked him for saving her and kissed him on the cheek. He blushed. She hopped into her father's van. The next thing Fear knew. Drake was walking over to him and handing him a duffle bag. He watched as the assassin unzipped the bag and peeked inside at all the dead presidents. He picked up one of the stacks, kissed it, and dropped it back inside of the bag. Smiling, he zipped the bag back up and tossed it onto the backseat.

"Thanks again," Drake told him and extended his hand.

Fear shook his hand and bid him a farewell. He watched as Drake jumped back inside the van with his security team and sped out of the parking lot.

Once the millionaire and his daughter were gone, Fear fired up his whip and looked to Constance. "So, where do you want me to drop you off, slim?" he inquired.

"I don't know. There aren't any shelters open at this hour," Constance informed him. "I guess I'll have to find a cheap motel to crash at or something."

"Wait a minute, you don't have any fam or nothing you can crash with? I mean, at least 'til you figure things out and get back on yo' feet?" he asked with a furrowed brow.

As far as he knew, everyone had family. Even if they didn't see eye to eye sometimes, they were still blood to you, and you should never hesitate to look out for them. Well, that's the way he thought it should be. Too bad, it didn't always work out that way for many people.

"Nah, I've been in the streets over half my life," Constance told him. "Even before then it was just me and my father. Although he was smoked out on crack, he was all I had, after my momma died."

"Damn." Fear looked through the windshield at nothing. He knew about loss at too well. The pain you felt due to losing a loved one hurt like a son of a bitch. He looked back over at Constance. "What happened to yo' moms?"

"She ran off with this cop and got married when I was just three-years-old," she told him sadly. Although she had a solemn look on her face, it caused her great heartache to rehash the story. "Me and my father never heard from her since then. No visits, no phone calls, no nothing. It was like as soon as he slid that ring on her finger, she vanished into the air. My father was so broken-hearted that he turned to crack to cope. That's how I ended up—" she tried to continue but she stopped herself. She was about to cry and the tears sting her eyes.

"How you ended up what?" Fear's face wrinkled with curiosity, and he adjusted himself in the seat.

Constance looked down, she shut her eyelids to stop shedding tears and bit down on her bottom lip. She had to get a grip on herself. She didn't want him to see her fall apart.

"Nothing." She shook her head and peeled her eyelids back open.

He could see the glassy look in her eyes, but he didn't want to comment on them. He knew she was hurt and probably didn't want to discuss it any further. He knew what that was like because he got like that sometimes too.

"Look, I know you don't know me from a hole in the wall, but if you could loan me some money, I swear on my life I'll pay you back. I ain't got one red cent to my name and I—" her words was cut short when Fear placed his finger to her lips.

He snatched the duffle bag off the backseat that Drake had given him. He opened it up and counted out four G-stacks. That was forty-thousand-dollars in cold, hard, tax-free cash, and he was going to give it all to her to have.

When Fear set the forty gees into Constance's lap, she couldn't help but cry then. She was overwhelmed by his generosity. She never had anyone bless her like this. Homeboy was so selfless. How could he drop a bag on her like this when he didn't know her or shit about her? For all, he knew she was going to run off with that money and never look back.

Sniffling, Constance wiped her eyes and licked her lips. She was trying to pull herself together so she could address Fear. Once she swallowed the spit in her throat, she composed herself enough to say something.

"Wait a minute, Fear. This is too much. It'll take me forever to pay you all of this back." She looked down at the stacks of money in her lap. "Here, I can't take this much from you." She tried to hand him the money back, but he pushed it back on her.

He wasn't having it. That bread was hers to keep and do with it as he pleased. "Nah, lil' mama, that's all you," Fear assured her. "I don't wanna dime of it back. Just make sure you do whatchu need to do to get back on yo' feet. If you wanna pay me back, you do it by looking out for someone like I looked out for you. Deal?" He looked her dead in her eyes.

Constance was speechless. She couldn't do anything but stare into his eyes as tears slid down her face. He was the most beautiful man she'd ever met. She felt like she was lucky to have crossed paths with him. She didn't know what came over her, but she lunged at him, grabbed him by the collar of his jacket, pulled him to her, and kissed him. She kissed him long, deep, and passionately. He was caught off guard at first, but he fell into it. Then, he realized he was engaged to Italia. How the fuck could he forget about her? She was the love of his life, and here his trifling ass was making out with another woman while she was laid up in the hospital on the account of him. What a dog ass nigga!

Fear's eyes exploded open, and he pulled away from Constance. She looked at him sorrowfully and wiped her mouth with her fingers.

"I'm sorry. I don't know what came over me," Constance admitted. "I guess I just got caught up in the moment."

"Nah, slim, it ain't chu," Fear confessed. "I'm engaged. And my lady is laid up in the hospital, right now. All cause of me at that." He shook his head pitifully. He was ashamed of himself for indulging in that kiss. Italia was his ride or die. She never made him question the love she had for him. So, he shouldn't be giving her reasons to question his, especially at a critical time like this.

"Oh," Constance said softly and looked out of the window. She felt like a goddamn fool. Although she'd just met Fear, she figured God had brought him into her life to love and cherish her. She really needed that with the situation she was in right now.

Goddamn it, I shoulda known it was too good to be true, especially with someone like me. I mean, how could a man as fine and as sweet as this love someone like me? I'ma whore! All of the niggaz that done ran through me, I can't even blame 'em. Lemme save face and get up outta here, I done embarrassed myself enough.

"Well, it's all good. No harm no foul." She presented him with a weak smile, then slipped the hoodie over her head he'd purchased from the 76-Gas station for her.

Afterward, she stuffed the pockets of it with the forty gees he'd given her and threw the hood on her head. Turning around to him, she kissed her fingertips and placed them against his cheek.

"Thank you, again," she told him before hopping out of the car and slamming the door shut.

He sunk low into his seat in deep thought, massaging his chin as he watched her stand at the traffic light. Her back was to him and her hands were inside of the pockets of her hoodie. If he had to guess, since they weren't too far from the Western Inn motel, she was going to get a room there for the night.

The traffic light turned green. Fear's eyes were glued to Constance as she made her way across the street with her head down. He didn't know what had gotten into him, but he started up his car and drove after her. He coasted alongside her trying his damndest to get her to get back in the car. No matter how hard he tried she brushed him off.

The truth was she was dying to get back in the car with him and go back to his crib. She was in love with his ass and hadn't even known him but a couple of hours. Although she wanted to give in to him, she was going to make him work a little bit harder for her compliance. She liked the thought of a man caring about her. She hadn't had that feeling since, well, she'd never had that feeling. All the men she dealt with only wanted her for her body and rightfully so. She was getting paid to fuck them so what else did she expect from them?

"Okay, fuck it. I'ma keep it one-thousand witchu, slim," Fear said, looking back and forth between the windshield and Constance. "I just moved into this new apartment and a nigga lonely as shit. I could really use the company. I think I'm going crazy. Shit, I'm tired of talking to myself," he poured it on thick. He didn't know it but as she walked down the sidewalk she was smiling. She loved the effort he was putting forth. "I mean, think about it. You could stay with me rent-free. You wouldn't have to spend a dime. Not even for food," he assured her. "You'll have your own bedroom, cable television, a frig fulla food. A hot bath!"

Suddenly, Constance whipped around to him and said, "Okay, I'm sold!" She ran to his car excitedly and hopped into the front passenger seat. She slammed the door shut and he drove off, grinning.

Hearing his cellular ringing, Fear looked at its display and saw it was his uncle Lester. He answered his call and they agreed to meet up.

"I'ma stop and holla at my unc before we go in. Cool?" Fear asked after disconnecting the call and sitting his cell phone aside.

"Cool." Constance flashed him a smile. She didn't care where they went as long as she got to spend time with him.

Chapter Three

Fear and Constance were sitting parked underneath the freeway. They engaged in small talk as they smoked a blunt between them. Their attention was drawn to the right of them when a black Lincoln Town Car pulled up ten feet away from them. Lester hopped out and jumped into the backseat of Fear's car.

"What's up?" Fear asked, looking into the rearview mirror at Lester.

"Nothing much," Lester answered. His eyes shifted to the back of Constance's head. His forehead wrinkled with curiosity. "Who's the broad?"

He'd always known Fear to roll solo.

"This is my homegirl, Constance. She's good people, I vouch for her," Fear assured him. His vouching of her let Lester know it was cool to talk around her.

Constance looked over her shoulder at Lester and threw her head back like, *What's up?* Lester returned the gesture. He didn't trust a fucking soul, but his nephew was solid. If he was putting his stamp of approval on lil' mama then she was good.

"Looka here, man, I'm sorry I couldn't make it to your mom's funeral." Lester affectionately gripped Fear's shoulder. "I got caught up in some shit. You did get the flowers and money I sent chu though, right?"

"Yeah, I got it. I appreciate it, family. It meant a lot." Fear locked eyes with Lester through the rearview mirror.

"Least I could do." Lester patted Fear on his shoulder. "It was a good move to have me up there guarding yo' lady. I caught a hitta up there trying to take her out. Mothafucka had a shot of poison he was trying to inject her with. I fixed his ass good, though," he assured him.

"Mothafucking Gustavo that had to be the only cocksucka to send 'em." Fear's face frowned angrily. He balled his fists tightly thinking of how Italia would have been killed if he hadn't sent his uncle to watch over her.

"It was definitely one of his guys," Lester assured him. "Once

I removed his get up, I recognized him from a photograph I saw at Gustavo's crib. If my memory serves me correctly, the kid was his nephew."

"Good looking out, unc."

"No problem, nephew. I'ma slide back up there once I finish hollering at chu," he assured him. "I gave orders to the front desk that they are to closely monitor her room, and not allow any visitors that aren't you or me." Lester unzipped his jacket and pulled out a manila envelope, passing it upfront to Fear. He watched Fear open the manila envelope and pull out a document, then closely look it over. "That's your boy Lethal that you told me to look up. His legal name is Ashton Yang Lee. I'm sure you already know that from news reports, though. Lil' yella motha-fucka has a rap sheet as long as my dick." Fear chuckled and shook his head as he continued to look over the document. "You should see where he's being held somewhere on there."

"Yeah, I see it," Fear confirmed wearing a serious expression.

He couldn't help thinking how much life was a trip. It turned out that old Lethal was being housed in the same facility as Gunplay. Fear was going to use this knowledge to his advantage. He was going to have Gunplay carve that ass up like a Christmas goose.

Uh-huh, mothafucka, every dog has his day and yours is com-ing very soon. Very, very soon, Fear thought as he slipped the document back inside the manila envelope and placed it in the flap of the sun-visor.

He pulled a small bankroll out of his pocket and handed it to Lester without looking over his shoulder at him. Lester thanked his nephew and stashed the bankroll inside his jacket.

"Yeah, nephew, I thought they were gonna have your boy in High Power considering all those bodies he dropped. But surpris-ingly he's in gen-pop, it seems to me like they want his ass dead," Lester informed him. "There's no telling who may be related to someone he popped at that funeral that will wanna get some get-back for their peoples."

Fear nodded as he listened to his uncle. He was right about

what he was saying. He hoped and prayed that if someone wanted to touch Lethal that they hadn't yet. He wanted to be the nigga indirectly responsible for his death since he couldn't be *the* one.

"You wanna know what else is crazy?" Lester asked, slipping his hands inside his jacket and looking at his nephew through the rearview mirror. Fear threw his head back like, *What's up?* "Gustavo wanted me to look into homeboy, too. It turns out he wants 'em dead."

Fear's forehead creased curiously. "Oh, yeah? Why is that?"

"Since he's gotten locked up on all of those murder beefs, he's become a liability to 'em. Homeboy feels he'll use 'em for a bargaining chip to save his ass from getting the needle. You know the needles coming for all those pigs he laid down."

"No doubt. Well, listen, if you planning to get someone to hit Lethal, I need you to throw that idea to the wayside," Fear told him, watching his reaction through the rearview mirror. "I gotta be the one that has this nigga's lights turned out. You feel me?"

Lester nodded, but he already set things in motion to have his young hitta behind the wall handle Lethal already. He was getting a fee for hooking Gustavo up and he wasn't about to let Fear's feelings get in the way of him making a dollar. Fuck that! He was going to keep his mouth shut and make sure he collected on that bag. He had to eat, and it was money over bullshit with him. Hell, he even had the shit inked on his shoulder. It was above a money bag with a dollar sign on it, so you'd know what he was about.

"Trip this shit, nephew, you're not gonna believe this." Lester chuckled. "Gustavo also wanted me to put the word out that he's put a two-hundred-fifty-thousand-dollar price tag on yo' head. Now, homie doesn't know we're related, so I asked 'em if I ran into you could I collect on it and he gave me the okay." Lester smiled devilishly at Fear through the rearview mirror.

It was from that *that* Fear knew he was going to blow his brains out and collect the bounty Gustavo had put on him. Keeping that in mind, Fear moved to draw his heat, but he was far too slow for the seasoned killa. Swiftly, Lester snatched two .45 automatic handguns with silencers from his jacket pockets. He pressed a gun each to the back of Fear and Constance's neck. Fear stiffened with his hand inside his jacket, where he had his handgun gripped. He kept his eyes on a scowling Lester wondering what move he was going to make next. He never thought his own blood would betray him in a million years, but he should have known better. Malik and Wameek had proven that blood isn't always thicker than water with their betrayal.

"I guess you came here to blow my shit back, so you can collect, huh? You ol' slimy fuck?" Fear's eyebrows arched and his nose scrunched up, hatefully.

"You bet your ass," Lester answered, keeping a close eye on Fear and Constance's every move. Their hearts thudded as they wondered what was going to come next. All they could hope for was a quick and painless death. "Sike." He smiled broadly and took the silencers from the back of Fear and Constance's neck, packing them back inside of his jacket. Fear and Constance sighed with relief and took a breath, thankful they didn't get their heads blown off. "It's family over everything. There isn't enough money in the world to make me cross my nephew. My lil' brother, Alvin, would turn over in his grave."

"Man, unc, I thought you were serious." Fear looked over his shoulder at him.

"Boy, I've been changing your shitty diapers since you were a baby. What the fuck do I look like putting a bullet in your head to collect a bag?" Lester questioned. He was kinda offended that his nephew would think he'd pop him for some bread. He'd be the first one to tell you he was a lot of things, but a snake wasn't one of them. "Now, blood or no blood, had you been a rapist, a pedophile, or a snitching piece-of-shit, I woulda gave you the business for that quarter, no lie."

"Same here, old head," Fear responded. "But chu ain't never gotta worry about cha boy eating the cheese."

Lester glanced at his watch before addressing Fear again. "Look, I gotta move I gotta make before I shoot back up there wit' cho girl. So, I'ma get up outta here."

"Alright, unc."

"You watch cho ass out here, A.J. And if shit gets too funky, don't hesitate to call me, okay?"

"Fa sho'."

"I love you, boy, take care." Lester looked through the driver's window at his nephew.

"I love you, too, unc. Good looking out on the info." Fear told him.

"You're welcome." He looked to Constance, waving goodbye. "You have a goodnight, baby girl."

"You, too," Constance threw up a hand. She looked to Fear. "So, you got two-hundred big ones on yo' head, huh?"

"Yeah," Fear said, watching Lester drive off. He then started up his car and drove off too. "I gotta come up with a game plan, or this nigga may actually succeed in getting my head knocked off my shoulders. He has far too many guns and funds for me to go at 'em on some solo shit. He's got the muscle on his side so I gotta use smarts. I gotta outthink this mothafucka if I'm gonna win."

"I hear you, and *we* will win. *We* will beat 'em," Constance assured, as she stared into his eyes and interlocked her fingers with his.

He looked down at her hand but didn't say anything. Although he knew he should have since he was engaged and still madly in love with Italia. It was hard for him to pull away. Since Italia had been gone, he'd been longing for the comfort of a woman, and Constance was providing that.

Fear looked at Constance and smiled. He liked the idea of someone having his back. Sure, he had his uncle, but it was something different knowing you had a down ass chick in your corner. The empowerment a woman could give a man couldn't be substituted by anything in the world. At least to him, it couldn't. Fear cranked up his whip and drove off, focusing his attention on the streets before him. Constance interlocked her fingers with his and his hand, affectionately. She then stared out the window and watched the streets pass her by in blurs. She loved the time she got to spend with Fear. But she knew once his fiancée got out of the hospital their time together would unfortunately end.

33

Constance's smile transformed into a scowl thinking about Italia coming between her and Fear. She slipped her fingers from between his and folded hers across her breasts. Fear's brows crinkled as he looked over at her, seeing her angry expression. He didn't know what had suddenly gotten into her, but he wasn't about to ask. He figured she was going through some emotional shit. That's what it was with most women.

These bitchez and their mood swings be killing me, boy. Fear shrugged and cranked the volume up on a *Rick Ross* CD. He then mashed the gas-pedal and zipped up the block, making his way on the freeway ramp, heading home.

***

Fear drove the stolen Dodge Challenger into the backyard of a house that was under construction. He whipped out two bandanas and passed one to Constance. Together, they wiped everything down being sure not to leave any fingerprints behind. Afterward, they caught a cab back to Fear's apartment complex. He made sure to tip the driver before they hopped out and descended to the tenement.

Once they got settled in Fear's apartment, he took a shower and got dressed for the night. He threw on a wave cap and a pair of black silk pajama pants. They were so low you could see the region of him that formed a V before you got to his bulging manhood. Constance was sitting on the living room couch, laughing her ass off and slapping her knee. She was watching *The Jefferson's* when Fear made his way across her, stealing a glance at the TV.

Constance couldn't help but see how well in shape he was. He had a muscular body that looked like it had been chiseled out of stone. Although his form was hideously scarred, she felt like it gave him crazy sex appeal, especially with his edgy attitude. He was giving her big dick energy. She could tell he was an educated street nigga by the way he carried himself, and that shit turned her on. In fact, it made her moist between her legs and gave her the urge to jump his bones.

Fear grabbed a bottle of Heineken out of the refrigerator. He took down a bag of pretzels from the cabinet and made his way out of the kitchen. He told Constance goodnight on his way to his bedroom, and she said it back to him. She licked her top lip as she watched his sculpted buttocks sway in his silk pajama pants. She didn't take her eyes off him until he disappeared inside his bedroom. She then grabbed the wife-beater, boxer-briefs, towels, toothpaste, and toothbrush he'd given her from the couch. Constance turned off the TV, before making her way to the bathroom.

Constance laid her items down on the toilet lid, turned on the hot shower water, and stepped inside the tub. She lathered herself up with Dove bodywash until she was milk-white from her neck down. She washed off the soap allowing the suds to slide down her shoulders, back, breasts, and incredibly flat stomach. Constance found herself playing between her thick thighs with triple X-rated thoughts of Fear dancing across her mind. Before she knew it, she was throwing her head back and hollering out, expressing her orgasm. Her eyes bulged, as she realized she'd gotten too loud. She slapped her hand over her mouth and looked around as if there was someone around to hear her. Taking note that she was alone, she finished her shower and turned off the dials.

Constance dried off, grabbed the pink bottle of Johnson & Johnson lotion, sat down on the toilet lid, and rubbed herself down with it from head to toe. Finishing, she slipped on a silk robe that matched with the pajama pants Fear was wearing that night. After she slipped it on, she tied it around her waist and nosily went through the pill bottles inside his medicine cabinet. Finding something that interested her, she took a few of the pills and placed the bottle back inside the cabinet. Next, she exited the bathroom pulling the door shut behind her. She journeyed down the hallway, stopped at his door, and made her way inside. She found him lying in bed sipping his beer and watching a rerun of Power.

His eyes darted over to her and all he could make out was her curvy silhouette. The sight of that alone made his dick jump. "What's up, slim? You good?" Fear inquired with his eyes glued to her.

The blue hue of the television illuminated Constance. He could see her partially now. She had this seductive look in her eyes. The way she licked her lips and bit down on her bottom one, made him feel like she was hungry for him. He loved that shit! It made him want to grab her, bend her over, and fuck the dog shit out of her.

"I've been thinking about all you've done for me," Constance told him as she slowly untied the silk robe. "And I'd like to pay you back." She slipped the robe off her shoulder. "In full." She allowed the robe to drop into a pile at her bare, manicured toes.

Fear found himself under the spell of her body as she slowly walked toward him. Constance had an hourglass shape. She also possessed full, perky tits with black areolas, and a bald pussy. Little mama had the body of an African goddess. It deserved to be worshipped by all its followers. Fear couldn't help biting down on his bottom lip and sliding his hands down his rock-hard abs. He was about to slip his hand inside his pants, but then he caught himself. He sat up in bed, cleared his throat, and composed himself. He was tripping allowing his little head to lead his big head. That wasn't how a man moved at all. He had to cut himself some slack, though. Homie hadn't had sex since Italia was laid up in the hospital, so he was quite vulnerable. No matter how strong he was mentally he was still a man, so his sexual needs were a part of his natural nature.

Fear couldn't find the words to convey what he needed to say to Constance. So, he ended up just staying quiet. He watched as she climbed into his bed and crawled toward him like a yellow, cat-eyed panther. Her locs were dangling in front of her face and she had a sensual look in her eyes. It was turning him on, but he was putting up a front like it wasn't. Constance gently took the Heineken bottle from him. She kept her eyes on him, as she licked up the neck of it, slid it inside of her pretty mouth, and slowly drank from it.

Still holding the bottle of beer, she stood up on her knees and wrapped her arms around his neck. He could smell the scent of alcohol on her breath, which carried a hint of minty toothpaste she'd brushed with earlier. She brushed her nose and lips against his to entice him. His hands had a mind of their own as they slipped around her waist. His head moved from left to right as his mouth was trying to press against hers for a kiss. She made sure to dodge him. This was her way of teasing him.

She was trying to get him riled up. It was working, too. It was driving him crazy. Again, he found his dick making the decisions for him, that he should have been letting his brain make. Without him having noticed, she'd slipped a few sleeping pills into his Heineken. She pushed him back on the bed and sat the bottle on his nightstand. She kissed him in the mouth, sucked on his bottom lip, and gently bit it.

Next, she worked her way down his body, tracing his old scars with her tongue, then kissing them tenderly. Glancing up at him, she saw his eyelids were shut and his mouth was stuck open. He was enjoying every minute of her foreplay. This brought a devilish smile to her lip. She smiled even harder when she felt his dick bulging against the fabric of his pajama pants.

Uh-huh, I know just how you like it, daddy, Constance thought as she continued down his abs and traced his six-pack with her tongue.

At this time, Fear's hands were tangled in her locs which were spilling between his fingers. He bit down on his bottom lip in anticipation of feeling her hot, moist mouth wrapped around his throbbing dick.

When I'm done with you, you'll be all mine. You won't even be able to think about another bitch, nor function without me. I'll be like crack and you'll be my fiend. How 'bout that?

Constance looked down and found a thin trail of hair that led down to Fear's dick. She grabbed a hold of his waistband and slowly began pulling his pajama pants down. She pulled his pants over his dick, and it leaped up at her. His shit was at its full length, with veins running up and down it. Clear, gooey, hot pre-cum oozed out of the pee-hole of his swollen mushroom tip. He was extremely aroused and aching to fill every single hole of hers.

Constance was definitely impressed with his length and girth. Although he wasn't that tall, he was definitely holding, and she couldn't wait to experience the talents he possessed. She grabbed his dick and gave it a little squeeze. It was slightly spongy, yet hard. Stroking him up and down, she watched as the skin of his meat wrinkled and straightened out. He was startled when his manhood finally met her mouth, sliding up and down it. Her hot saliva spilled down his piece like an avalanche, coating it. Her head bobbed up and down. She made gagging and slurping noises spilling more and more of her hot saliva down his shaft. He gripped her head. Her head game was nice and nasty, just how he liked it.

Constance sucked and jerked him off simultaneously for ten minutes straight. When she pulled her head back there was a string of saliva hanging from her bottom lip like rope. The opposite end of it was attached to his dick. She twirled it around her fingers, and it glistened in the light of the television. She looked at it like it was fascinating, before putting it back on his piece.

Constance wiped her mouth with the back of her hand. She then harped up some mucus and spat on his dick. She got back to work, using her mouth and both of her hands, she sucked the head of his shit while jerking him up and down. He threw his head back and groaned in pleasure. His eyelids were squeezed shut, and he was basking in the moment.

Fear started moaning like a straight-up bitch. Constance had some head that was out of this world. She had a nigga feeling like he was on another planet. His face balled up tight and he began grunting, face fucking her with his eyes shut. Her gags and her saliva swishing around inside her mouth excited him. The shit was driving him crazy! His breathing became heavier as he neared his nut, feeling his semen expand the girth of his piece. Peeling his eyes open, he was stunned to see Italia standing by the door of his bedroom.

The sight of her startled him and zapped his cum right back down into his nut sack. He backed up into the headboard on the palms of his hands. He blinked his eyes once and peeled them back open, Italia had disappeared. His head whipped all around his bedroom, but she wasn't anywhere in sight.

"What's wrong?" A confused Constance asked while wiping the excess spit from around her mouth. She looked around the bedroom trying to see if she could see whatever he was looking for. There wasn't anything in sight, though so she focused her attention back on him. "Fear, tell what's the matter?" She cupped his face in her hands and looked him into his eyes.

He continued to scan the bedroom but coming up with nothing. Finally, he shut his eyes briefly and took a deep breath. Peeling his eyes back open, he focused on the look of concern on Constance's face. Slowly, he pulled her hands from off his face.

"I thought—I thought I saw her," Fear stammered, breathing heavily.

You would have thought he'd seen a ghost. Truthfully, the thought of Italia catching him cheating terrified him. He didn't want to cause her the emotional pain that kind of heartbreak would surely bring. He knew it would hurt her and what hurt her would devastate him—greatly.

Oh, fuck, not this bitch again! Constance thought, dropping her head, then looking back up at him. She was disappointed because she really wanted to get it in with him. The thought of his fiancée was really cramping her style.

"I'm sorry. I'm really not tryna lead you on," Fear told her. "It's just that—it's just that since my fiancée has been in the hospital—it's been a while since I've been touched by a woman or been intimate. I can't front, a nigga kinda miss that feminine touch." He took a deep breath before continuing. "I gotta learn how to control my dick before I fuck around and not just hurt my boo, but you as well."

"Well, if it's the touch of a woman you miss, I can lay in your arms and we could just talk," Constance told him. Though she wanted to be fucked and not held, she'd settled for cuddling with him.

"Are you straight with that?" Fear questioned with a raised eyebrow, trying to make sure she was comfortable with doing that.

He was sure he wasn't about to let his dick do his thinking for him this go around. So, if Constance was going to try him again she was going to be sorely disappointed. He wasn't going to give in to his sexual urges again. He loved Italia too much to risk hurting her and losing her forever.

"Yeah," Constance replied.

He opened his arms and she lay against him, feeling his big strong arms wrap around her. She never felt so safe in all the years she'd been alive. She didn't know what it was about him, but she felt protective at all times. It was like he was her guardian angel. "So, talk to me, tell me about you. What's your story?"

"You wanna know a nigga's history, huh?" He grinned and glanced down at her. She smirked and nodded. He took a deep breath and laid his head back against the headboard. Afterward, he went on to tell her his life's story, leaving out all the murders he'd committed. He wasn't foolish enough to give anyone any information that could get him locked up for the rest of his life.

"Wow, you've been through a lot of shit," Constance said. She was amazed with everything Fear had gone through, especially with him coming from such a well-off family. She knew that nearly every tragedy he met was on account of his involvement with the streets. She couldn't help wondering if he regretted his decision to become a street nigga. Although she wondered, she wasn't about to ask him. The last thing she wanted was for him to feel bad about the choices he'd made. Or feel responsible for the many deaths the path he chose brought, even if those lives rested solely on his shoulders.

"We've all gotta sob story."

"True indeed."

"I'd like to hear yours if you care to share."

Constance took a deep breath as she stared ahead at nothing. She didn't know exactly where to start in her story. So, she figured she'd just close her eyes and think of the saddest time in her life and begin there.

Tranay Adams

Chapter Four

Thirteen-year-old Constance stood on a folding chair, duct-taping a black garbage bag over a broken window. The window had been smashed in earlier that night. Constance had come back from panhandling to find a homeless man trying to get inside. She deepened her voice so it would carry like an older man's and it spooked him. He dropped the brick he'd used to shatter the window and took off running.

Situations like this were a normal occurrence for Constance and her father, Radcliff. There was always someone trying to break inside their home. Before they had moved into the house functioned as a sanctuary for homeless people. They'd crash there when they needed a place to sleep or consume their drugs. The place used to reek of urine and feces, but Constance and her old man cleaned it up as best they could. It still smelled funny but at least the odor was tolerable. They'd brought in an old, worn-out couch and La-Z-Boy reclining chair someone had discarded outside on the curb. An elderly couple that Radcliff did landscaping and other household chores for, gave them a coffee table, a couple of lamps, twin bunk beds, among other things.

Now the house was a far cry from the presidential suite at the Ritz. The inside thanks to Radcliff and Constance was decent at best. But the outside, well, that was another story altogether. There was graffiti sprawled on the outside of the house and all windows were boarded up. The front and backyard lawns were unkempt. The grass had died, and the weeds had grown up to Constance's waist. Still, you could tell Constance and her old man lived in the mother of all shitty houses. She was fine with that. The way she looked at it, living there was a lot better than sleeping inside a tent out on Skid Row.

Once Constance had finished taping the garbage bag over the window, she jumped down from the folding chair and set it aside. She reached behind the tattered sofa and withdrew a wooden baseball bat. Her father had hammered nails into it so it would make for a formidable weapon. They kept it stashed behind the sofa for security purposes. You know, in case, some assholes broke in and wanted to steal what little valuables they had.

Constance gripped the baseball bat and practiced swinging it, imagining defending herself against burglars. Smelling her pot of Pork n Beans cooking, she placed the baseball bat back where she'd stashed it. She speed-walked over to the kitchen counter where she had the pot of beans cooking on a single burner. She turned the burner off, picked up her pot of beans, and grabbed a big wooden spoon. Constance scooped up some of the beans and cautiously tasted them. They were hot and she didn't want to risk burning her mouth. Feeling a burning sensation on the tip of her tongue, she set the pot back on the burner and decided to let the beans cool off.

It was cold as hell in the house, so Constance had to dress extra warm. She was in a beanie, two sweaters, and a burgundy hoodie. Still, she found herself blowing her hot breath into her hands and rubbing them together to keep warm. She threw her hood on her head and grabbed the blanket off the bottom bunk. She swung the blanket around her shoulders like a cape as she walked back inside the living room.

Constance walked over to the twenty-inch boxed television set on the blue milk crate. It was scarred up, one of its antennas was bent, and its top dial was missing. She pressed the on button on the T.V. and it popped on. She used the butter knife lying on top of the milk crate to turn to the channel she desired. The television screen had lines of static dancing across it, so she adjusted its antennas until the picture was clear.

Constance sat Indian-Style on the floor and watched a rerun of The Jefferson's. She threw her head back laughing and slapped her knee repeatedly. At that moment she was happy her father had run an extension cord to the neighbor's house. They were able to siphon juice from them and provide their entire home with electricity.

Boom! Boom! Boom! Boom!

Someone's pounding at the backdoor startled Constance from her T.V. show. Wondering who it was, she sprung to her feet and grabbed the baseball bat from behind the sofa. She cautiously approached the kitchen with the baseball held up at her shoulder. The pounding at the backdoor seemed to grow louder and louder the closer she got to it. She stopped a few feet away from the backdoor and swallowed a lump of fear.

This couldn't be daddy. He usually doesn't come back 'til the wee hours of the morning, when he's out hustling to get his fix, Constance thought as she tightened her grip on the baseball bat.

At one time her father, Radcliff was a man of the cloth, a minister at a very prominent church. He had a huge following and they loved him like he was God Almighty. It wasn't until he lost his wife, Shyia to a mugging gone wrong that he lost his faith in his religion. He turned his back on the holy gospel and his noble men and women turned their backs on him.

Unable to cope with the loss of his better half, Constance's mother, and his congregation, Radcliff turned to crack cocaine. Although the drug eased his suffering, it blinded him to everything else that was falling apart around him. It wasn't long before he found himself and his daughter soliciting and stealing to survive. Still, their circumstances didn't stop Radcliff's craving for crack. He spent most of his days doing odd jobs and hustling in the streets to get up the money he needed to purchase drugs. A lot of times Constance didn't see him for days at a time and she'd have to fend for herself.

"Who is it?" Constance called out nervously.

"It's—it's me, baby! It's your daddy!" Radcliff answered with a panic-stricken voice. She could tell by the way he sounded that something was terribly wrong. "Open the door, baby girl, hurry up!"

Constance lowered her baseball bat and hurriedly opened the backdoor. Radcliff rushed inside, slamming the door, and locking it. He darted over to the kitchen window and peered through its curtains. He didn't see anyone following him. Radcliff took in a gulp of air and turned around to his daughter, panting. His face was hot, sticky, and sweaty.

"Daddy, what happened? What's going on?" Constance

asked concerned.

She had a look of worry across her face, especially when she took in her father's appearance. He had a bloody nose and busted lip. A knot the size of an 8-ball was on his forehead. It was obvious he'd been in a fight or had been jumped. She just didn't know what it pertained to.

Radcliff took the baseball bat from Constance before making sure the backdoor was secure. Although it was, it was raggedy as a mothafucka! Anyone on the outside wouldn't have any trouble getting through it if they applied enough pressure.

Radcliff told Constance about a kilo of cocaine he'd stolen. The nigga he'd stolen it from was now after him. He and a white girl had jumped out on him while he was fishing recyclables from out of the garbage.

"The next thing I knew the white broad took off on me and I fell to the ground. I tried to get up but that ol' pretty pimping ass nigga kicked me in my ribs," Racliff told her. "They both started punching, kicking and stomping me while I was down. Then dude pulled a gun out on me. He tried to shoot me in my head, but his piece jammed up on 'em. As soon as that happened I knew I hadda get the hell up outta there. So I shoved the white broad outta the way and took flight down the street—hauling all one-hundred and thirty-two pounds of my skinny, black poor-ass."

"Well, daddy, why don't chu just give 'em back his drugs? Maybe he'll leave you alone," Constance told him.

"Baby girl, that dope is long gone. My homeboy and I smoked that brick weeks ago," Radcliff regretfully informed her.

"Damn, daddy, an entire kilo of cocaine?" Constance asked with disbelief. She couldn't believe he'd smoked up that much. She'd seen a kilo of coke in movies before and if the one he had was anywhere near that size then that was a lot. A lot more than she felt he could have smoked up by himself.

"Yeah, an entire kilo, I didn't smoke the shit up myself," Radcliff reported, which was starting to make sense to Constance. "It was me and Clarence ass getting high together. As a matter of fact, I bet that's how that nigga and that white broad knew we'd

*stolen their shit. Ol' big blabber mouth-ass Clarence, that cracked-out-cocksucka gotta tell everything he knows. Goddamn!"
Furious, he bit down on his bottom lip, kicking and swinging on the air. "I swear before God when I catch up to that there big head nigga I'ma beat 'em like he's a runaway slave." He swore. What he didn't know was the mysterious young couple had already caught up with his boy Clarence and put a bullet in his head. So old Radcliff would never be able to give him that ass beaten he'd promised.*

"Daddy, who is it?"

"Who's who? The nigga that's after me?"

"Yeah, who is he?"

"Draymond."

At the mention of the name, Draymond a shocked look came over Constance's face. The color drained from her face, her eyes bulged, and her mouth flung open. She looked like she'd seen a ghost. You see, everybody knew exactly who Draymond was and if they didn't, then they'd at least heard some spooky stories about him. He was talked about like the Boogie Man on the account of the work he put in on the streets. The man was twenty-five-years-old, and he was already a legend in the game. He dealt in pussy, heroin, and crack cocaine. Draymond was definitely a nigga you wouldn't want to cross because you'd pay for it with your life.

Boom!

The backdoor rattled from a tremendous force that startled Constance and her father. They whipped around to the backdoor with spooked looks on their face. Radcliff pulled his daughter behind him, gripped the baseball bat, and raised it up to his shoulders.

"Stay behind me, baby girl, shit just got real." A terrified Radcliff swallowed the lump of fear in his throat. Constance held his waist with one hand and peered from the side of him. Her eyes were glossy and she was afraid.

Boom!

Chapter Five

The door flung open and splinters flew everywhere. A white broad with fire, red hair crossed the threshold into the kitchen first. She was average looking with long eyelashes and red matte lipstick painted lips. Her balloon breasts were too big for her body and were obviously surgically enhanced. She was wearing a black, leather, form-fitting skirt that showcased her cleavage. Her black, leather, hooker boots displayed her thick, juicy thighs. She lifted her .32 pistol and pointed it at Radcliff.

"Aaaahhh!" Constance screamed terrified.

As the white broad, Cherry pulled the trigger of her pistol, Radcliff swung his bat. The baseball bat swooshed as it soared through the air, connecting with Cherry's hand as her small-caliber pistol fired. The pistol flew across the kitchen and ricocheted off the wall, landing upside down against it.

"Ah, you motherfucker!" Cherry mad dogged Radcliff as she rubbed her aching hand. "You're going to pay for that, you fucking crack fiend!" she swore with flaring nostrils and clenched jaws.

"Indeed, he will," a deep baritone voice rang out, drawing everyone's attention.

They looked to the doorway and found a tall, dark figure. Radcliff and Constance hadn't identified the presence lurking in the shadows yet, but an icy chill ran down their spines. They knew it was the man, the monster, the devil himself, Draymond.

Radcliff and Constance slowly stepped back as the dark figure walked inside the kitchen. The closer he came, the more of him was revealed, until they could view him in his entirety. Draymond was a handsome man with an athletic physique. He had light-brown eyes and coffee-brown skin. His silky black hair spilled from beneath his purple fedora and lay over his broad shoulders. He wore a perfectly tailored suit underneath a black chinchilla fur coat.

"It's time to pay the piper, Mr. Smith." Draymond's face scrunched up angrily and he balled his fists.

Figuring it was now or never, Radcliff charged at him and swung the baseball bat with all his might. Draymond duck the swing of the bat that would have taken his head off had it connected. Radcliff followed up by taking several more swings at him which he avoided easily. The last swing came for his head; he bent at the waist and ducked it. When he came back up, he kicked Radcliff in his chest, and he went flying into the living room. He dropped his baseball bat while in midair and crashed to the carpeted floor, wincing.

Constance became furious seeing her father assaulted. She charged at Draymond swinging wildly. He avoided her attack with his fluid movements and backhanded her in true pimp fashion. Constance spun around in midair dramatically before hitting the floor. She was dazed, confused, and bleeding at the mouth.

"You've got some heart, lil' nigga, but chu not ready to slap-box with the God." Draymond looked down at Constance pitifully.

Once Cherry recovered her .32, she stepped behind him and slipped off his fur coat. Draymond thanked her and unbuttoned the single button of his suit's jacket. He started toward the living room where Radcliff had turned on his side, holding his aching back. Draymond pressed his black leather dress shoe onto his throat and applied pressure. Radcliff's face balled up in pain, as he clutched the pimp's ankle with both hands.

"Now, where the fuck is my kilo of coke?" Draymond asked through clenched jaws and hostile eyes.

"It's—it's gone—" Radcliff gagged as he felt his windpipe being crushed. The veins on his forehead bulged and his eyes watered.

"Wrong answer!" Draymond snatched his foot from Radcliff's neck. Radcliff lifted his back from the floor holding his neck and coughing harshly. Constance ran inside of the living room and got down on her knees, comforting her father. "Cherry, put one in this smoked out ass nigga so we can get the fuck outta here, ma."

"Yes, daddy," Cherry laid his fur coat across the arm of the sofa and approached Radcliff. She was about to blow his brains out in front of his daughter.

Constance looked back and forth between Draymond and Cherry. She was scared for her father. She didn't want him to be killed. He was all she had in the world since her mother was gone. "No! Wait, please, don't kill him! Please!" she pleaded with Draymond. "However much he owes you we'll pay you back—double!"

"Do you know how much a brick cost? And you're talking about hitting my hand with double that? We're talking, like, fifty gees, lil' homie," Draymond informed. "I don't know if you've noticed, but your old man's a fucking crackhead. I'd like to quote the late, great, Notorious B.I.G, 'you think a crackhead paying you back, forget it'. If yo man can't gimme what he owes me right this minute, he's a dead man. It's as simple as that!" Draymond threw up his hand and snapped his fingers, addressing Cherry. "Gon' and handle yo business, baby."

Cherry pointed her pistol at Radcliff's head, and he raised his trembling hands. His eyes were still watering from being choked out. "Wait, wait, I can give you something. I can give you something, right now," he assured him.

Draymond looked all around the living room. Everything that Radcliff believed was valuable was junk to him. He looked back at the crackhead like he was crazy, saying, "Nigga, please, there isn't shit in this filthy mothafucka worth the bread you owe me. You can't be serious."

"How about her?" Radcliff placed his hand on Constance's shoulder.

She looked at him and her heart split in half. Tears instantly spilled down her cheeks. Her mouth hung open in shock. She couldn't believe the only person in the world she thought cared about her was trying to give her away. At that moment, she didn't feel human. She felt like a piece of property.

"I'm—I'm sorry, baby girl," Radcliff looked at her sorrowfully.

Constance wiped her dripping eyes with her curled finger and sniffled. The emotional pain she felt right then was worse than any physical pain she'd ever felt.

"Sorry, but I don't deal in dick, I deal in pussy." Draymond informed him. "Cherry, pop this nigga!" Cherry went to shoot him, and he spoke up again, stopping her.

"No, wait, she is a girl," Radcliff assured him.

He stood up and pulled Constance to her feet. Her head was bowed, and she was at a loss for words. She was so hurt that she didn't even have the strength to put up a fight. It was like her willingness to live had been zapped out of her.

Radcliff snatched the hood off Constance's head and then pulled off her beanie. Her neck lengths locs spilled out and hung loosely.

"See?" He looked back and forth between Draymond and Constance.

He hoped the pimp was willing to take his daughter in exchange for the brick he'd stolen. Although he knew that he was as wrong as two left shoes for what he was doing, the way he figured, Constance's lifelong servitude to a flesh peddler, was better than him having to lose his life.

Draymond's brows furrowed and he stared at Constance curiously, tilting his head aside. "Well, I'll be damned. All this time I thought lil' mama was a lil' ass boy." He approached Constance and held up her chin, looking into her face.

She had a beautiful face and the prettiest eyes he'd ever seen in his life. Constance shut her eyes and tears rolled from the corners of her eyes. Her bottom lip quivered, but he didn't give a fuck. He had to be reimbursed for his loss. "How old is she? About ten?"

"Hell naw, man, she's thirteen!" Radcliff told him like her being three more years older made a difference. She was still a minor no matter how he looked at it.

When Radcliff gave Constance's correct age Draymond's head whipped around to him. The fact that he sounded so excited about selling his own daughter made Draymond sick to his stomach. He started to reach over his shoulder and smack his bitch-ass like he would one of his bitchez. But he had to look at this delicate situation through the eyes of a businessman. Radcliff's loss would be his gain. Besides, he'd have to be the one that would have to live with the choice he'd made.

"Before we enter into any agreement. I'm gonna have to inspect the merchandise if you know what I mean," Draymond told Radcliff.

"Sure. Yeah. I understand. Go right ahead." Radcliff stepped aside.

The moment he did, the pimp gave his down-ass-bitch the signal to lower her gun, to which she did.

"Take your clothes off for me, lil' mama," Draymond told Constance. Constance slowly began taking off all her layers of clothing until she was in a dingy white bra and panties. "Remove your bra and panties, too. I need to see what my dope is buying." Constance stared up at him defiantly. She wanted to fight him, but she knew the odds weren't in her favor. He was a grown-ass man, so he was naturally stronger than her. Plus, Cherry was strapped, and she knew she wouldn't hesitate to pop her ass. "I'm not gonna repeat myself," he gave her a stern warning.

Constance's cheeks flooded with tears as she undid her bra, freeing her two handfuls of breasts. She flung her bra aside and placed her arm over her underdeveloped boobs. She bent at the waist and slipped off her panties, flinging them aside as well. She then placed her hand over her vagina to shield it from everyone's prying eyes.

"Remove your hands, so I can see all of you," Draymond ordered.

More tears flowed down Constance's cheeks as she took her arm from her breasts and removed her hand from between her legs. Draymond motioned with his finger for her to spin around for him. Constance slowly spun around feeling degraded. Right then, she promised herself she'd never forgive her father. He could never make this right with her, no matter what he did.

Draymond's eyes were narrowed and focused on Constance as he massaged his chin. He was taking in all of her. She stopped her spin and found herself standing in front of him. He walked around her massaging his chin, ogling her, and thinking.

This lil' bitch gotta young, tight, nice body. I know I can make a pretty penny with her. She'll be the top earner in my stable fa sho', Draymond thought, as he continued to check out Constance's underage merchandise. "Lil' mama, are you a virgin?"

"What? Of course, she's a—"

Draymond threw his hand up which killed off whatever Radcliff was saying. He looked him in his eyes and balled up his face, clenching his jaws. "Mothafucka, I'm not talking to you. How the fuck you gon' tell me what she does with her pussy? I'm pretty sure you spend most of your time chasing your high than you do paying her any attention."

Radcliff lowered his head and fidgeted with his fingers. He couldn't say shit. Draymond's good pimping ass was right. He was so caught up in getting high that he hardly paid Constance any attention.

"Just like I thought. Open your mouth again, and I'll smack the taste out of it. You understand me?" Radcliff looked up at him pitifully and nodded. "Lil mama, so tell me what's up. You still holding onto that V-card?" he questioned Constance.

"Yeah, I'ma virgin." She answered timidly.

"Alright, I'ma have to break you in then. Trick's aren't gonna pay top dollar for some pussy they've gotta break into the game. I've had my share of green bitchez. Lemme tell you, the shit isn't fun. All of that whining and blood everywhere. A mothafucka that's spending good money doesn't wanna deal with all that bullshit." Draymond put his hands on his hips and took another good look at Constance. He took a deep breath and nodded. "Alright, Radcliff, you've got yourself a deal."

A smile stretched across Radcliff's face and he jumped for joy excited, pumping his fist into the air. He ran over to Draymond and shook his hand with both of his. "Oh, thank you! Thank you! Thank you, Draymond. This is one deal you won't live to regret. Trust and believe me. My girl's gonna make you a lot of paypa," he assured him. "You're gonna be swimming in cash like Scrooge McDuck."

Draymond smiled weakly at Radcliff. He then wiped his hand

*off on his pants. Radcliff was an old musty-ass nigga, so he knew
he was dirty. He didn't want his rank ass touching any parts of
him.*

"Go ahead and put your clothes back on, lil' mama," Draymond told Constance. Quickly, she slipped her clothes back on
and pulled her beanie down over her head.

Radcliff whipped around to Constance as she was mad dogging him. Her nose was flaring and tears were consistently sliding
down her face. The smile slowly retracted from Radcliff's lips
seeing how sad and hurt she was. He placed his hands on her
shoulders and bowed his head, clearing his throat. He looked back
up at her with serious eyes.

"Baby girl, I know you think what I did was fucked up. But
you see I'm not fit to take care of you," Radcliff admitted. "I
mean, look at how we're living. Trust me. You'll live a much better
life with this man. A far better life than you have living with me.
Hell, the way I see it, you should be thanking me right—"

Constance spat a thick glob of mucus in Radcliff's face. He
shut his eyes as it slowly slid down his nose and dripped off the tip
of it. He took a deep breath as he pulled out a folded handkerchief
from his back pocket. He wiped the gooey glob off his face and
nodded, slipping the handkerchief into his back pocket. Nodding,
he said, "I deserve that. I can admit—"

Smack! Constance's hand flew across Radcliff's face in a blur
and whipped his head around.

His cheek was left stinging and a red hand impression was left
on it. He looked back at her, holding his cheek with a surprised
look on his face. He looked like he wanted to choke her ass to
death, but the look she gave him, told him she'd kill him if he tried
her.

"Let's go, daddy," Constance told Draymond as she walked
away from her father.

"Not just yet, lil' mama, your father, and I have some business
we need to wrap up," Draymond told her with his eyes glued on
Radcliff.

The crackhead's face balled up with confusion. He didn't

know what the hell the pimp was talking about. "What—what do you mean?" Radcliff asked. He started to worry, and his heart raced. His hands became clammy and he started sweating. He feared the worse was to come and he was absolutely right. "We hadda—we hadda deal."

"We still do." Draymond stepped to Radcliff, smirking devilishly. "There are just a few stipulations in the contract."

"What stipulations?" Radcliff wondered with a raised eyebrow.

"Oh, don't tell me you didn't read the fine print?" Draymond told him. He snapped his fingers and Cherry appeared at his side, pistol in hand.

She kicked Radcliff in his balls, and he doubled over, holding himself. She then whacked him upside the head, and he fell to the floor. Once she tucked her .32, she continued to stomp and kick Radcliff. Surprisingly, Constance joined in on the action, stomping and kicking him also. Radcliff hollered out as he was brutally punished.

"You know what they do to niggaz they catch stealing in third world countries, Radcliff? They chopped off the hand they were caught stealing with. Now, I don't have a clue as to what hand you used to lift my key. But I noticed you extended your left-hand first when you went to shake mine. That means you're a lefty." Draymond announced his discovery. He'd hit the nail on the head too.

Draymond tossed his hat on the La-Z-Boy. He pulled his hair back into a ponytail and tangled a rubber-band around it. While he was doing this, he watched as Cherry and Constance beat the dog shit out of Radcliff. He pulled a machete from the small of his back, where it was sheathed, walked over to the coffee table, and knocked everything from off it with it. Draymond pulled the coffee table into the center of the living room floor; he sat his machete on top of it and unbuckled his leather belt. He pulled the belt free from the loops of his pants and turned to Cherry and Constance.

"Y'all drag that bitch-ass nigga over here!" Draymond motioned Cherry and Constance over with the hand he held his belt

in.

He watched as the girls dragged a battered and bruised Radcliff towards him. Radcliff's face was covered in blood like he'd dunked his head into a bucket of it. One of his eyes was swollen shut, and the other one had two blood clots in it. His nose was broken and crooked, so he was wheezing every time he breathed. The air coming from his nose made an eerie whistling sound. Radcliff was in a world of hurt, moaning, and groaning.

"Remove his coat and roll his sleeve up to his elbow. Then, outstretch his arm across the table." Draymond watched as his bitchez did like he'd told them. Once they were done, he looped his belt around Radcliff's arm, pulled it tight, and buckled it. "Baby, hold this cocksucka's arm down and make sure he doesn't move."

"Yes, daddy," Cherry and Constance replied in unison.

Draymond took the time to remove his suit's jacket and unbuttoned his button-down shirt. He slipped out of them and tossed them on the arm of the sofa. Draymond pulled his wife-beater from over his head and tossed it on the rest of his clothing also. His body was littered with keloids from neglected gunshot wounds.

Draymond walked around the coffee table tapping the dull side of his machete into his palm, eyes fixated on Radcliff's outstretched arm. He took a few steps back, swung the machete above his head, and brought it down with all his might. The machete went through flesh, muscle, tendon, and bone.

Chomp!

Chapter Six

As soon as the machete met Radcliff's arm, his eyeballs nearly popped out of his head and his mouth stretched open far and wide. "Aaaaaaaaah!"

The machete had only gotten halfway through Radcliff's arm. Draymond was having trouble pulling it back out, so he placed his foot on his shoulder and pulled it free. Again, he swung the machete back over his head and brought it down with all his might. This time, the machete went through Radcliff's arm and buried itself into the coffee table.

"Aaaaaahhh!" Radcliff screamed at the top of his lungs, displaying his yellowish, rotten, and missing teeth. He lifted his severed arm and blood squirted out of two different areas before it dripped out onto the carpeted floor.

Draymond pointed his machete at Radcliff and said, "Cherry, shut 'em up! Shut 'em the fuck up!"

Cherry slipped off her panties and stuffed them inside of Radcliff's mouth, clamping her hand over his lips to stifle his screams. Draymond sat his machete down on the coffee table and walked over to the burner that Constance's pot of beans was sitting on. He pulled a bandana out of his back pocket, grabbed the pot by its handle, and dumped its contents out onto the floor. As he turned around a fat ass gray rat scurried by his dress shoes, but he didn't notice it. He continued his way toward Radcliff watching him struggle to escape the clutches of his women.

"Hold his arm up!" Cherry and Constance did as they were instructed.

Draymond placed the bottom of the pot against Radcliff's stump. There was a loud sizzling sound, like something hot being dipped into water. The smell of burning flesh filled the air, as the bottom of the hot pot, burned the bleeding end of Radcliff's stump closed.

Cherry and Constance helped Draymond get dressed. The pimp hung his arm on Constance's neck and led her toward the backdoor. She suddenly stopped and looked at Radcliff. He lay on the floor bawling and looking up at her shamefully. He didn't know it, but he'd broken a part of her she'd never be able to fix. Draymond continued to lead Constance toward the kitchen, where they exited the backdoor.

Cherry drove the black-on-black 2011 Cadillac Escalade truck into the backyard of Draymond crib. Cherry and Constance hopped out of the SUV. Constance stood aside and Cherry opened the backdoor. Draymond eased out the back of the truck and Cherry closed the door behind him. He was talking to someone on his cell phone. He told them to hold on and told Cherry to fix Constance up for her initiation. Cherry grabbed Constance's hand and led her into the house through the backdoor.

"Yeah, I gotta new booty over here," Draymond spoke into his cellular. "Nah, this one is new-new. She's gotta be broken in, and you know how I hate doing that shit. So, gather some of your boys and slide on through. Yeah, I'm having my Snow Queen fix her up now. Alright, now, I'll politic wit' chu when you get here." Draymond disconnected the call and stashed his cellular.

He proceeded over to the gated kennel he kept his two pit-bulls behind. They both were big-headed and muscular. One was golden brown and had a pink nose. The other was gray and had a blue nose. The beasts were two mean old bastards, fitting to be the lapdogs of Satan.

The pit-bulls barked and jumped up and down on the kennel's gate. They were happy to see their master and he was happy to see them, too.

"Hey, y'all! Y'all missed daddy, huh? Didn't you? Didn't you miss, daddy?" Draymond talked to the beasts like they were a couple of toddlers. He was more kind and loving to his hounds than his whores. "You hungry? Are my babies hungry? Daddy's got something for you." He reached deep inside the recesses of his fur coat and pulled out something wrapped in a bloodstained white cloth.

He unfolded the cloth and revealed Radcliff's severed hand. The pit-bulls grew excited at the smell of fresh blood. They could not wait to sink their fangs into the human flesh. Draymond teased the dogs with Radcliff's hand before tossing it over inside the kennel. The blue-nosed one snagged it out of the air. He and the golden-brown pit played tug-of-war with it until they pulled it in half. They then went to their separate corners and started chomping away.

Draymond smiled at his vicious pets before heading inside his house. He hung his hat and stripped down to his wife-beater. He put the sheathed machete up in the cabinet above the refrigerator, took his plate of heroin out of the refrigerator, and walked it over to the table. He sat down and picked up the rolled dollar bill. Then he placed the rolled bill to his right nostril, pressed his left nostril closed, and hunched over the plate, snorting up one of the three lines of Boy.

"Whoooo!" Draymond said cheerfully as he threw his head back. He was enjoying the feeling of euphoria the heroin brought.

It had him as right as rain. Thinking he was about to sneeze he pinched his nose closed so he wouldn't waste the good dope. When he brought his head back down, he was teary-eyed, and his nose was dripping. He sniffled and pulled on his nose.

"All done," Cherry announced proudly from over Draymond's shoulder. He turned around to find her standing behind Constance with her hands on her shoulders. "What do you think?"

Constance's locs had been tightened and greased. Her face was beat to the Gods. Her makeup made her look like a little girl trying to look like a grown woman. She had on a black, sheer, teddy with the matching coat to match, and pumps with the black fur on them. You could see her premature lady parts.

Draymond cracked a one-sided grin and started applauding. "Good job, slim. Did you lace her?"

"Yeah. I filled her in on everything, daddy," Cherry assured him.

As Draymond's bottom-bitch Cherry was assigned the task of showing the new girls the game. She taught them everything from how to entice men and getting them to spend more with them, to the amount of money they were to bring to the table each week. She even let them know what would happen should they ever break any of daddy's rules.

"That's a good bitch." Draymond looked to Constance and motioned her over.

She stood in front of him, trying desperately to keep her balance in her pumps. Once she was standing upright, he took another look at her and could see she was visibly nervous. She was trembling, her knees were knocking, and she looked really uncomfortable.

"Come over here and sit on daddy's knee, lil' mama." He patted his knee. She sat down on it and he combed his fingers through her locs, admiring her beauty. "You scared, huh?" Constance hesitantly nodded. "Everything is gonna be all right, mama. I'ma give you a lil' something, something that'll set chu straight so you can handle yo business. Cherry, fix lil' mama a drink, straight up," he told her, and she went off to make the drink he requested.

Once she was busy whipping up the alcohol beverage, he passed Constance the rolled dollar bill, demonstrating to her how to snort up the heroin. Constance didn't really want to try the drug for fear she'd fuck around and get hooked on it like her father. She also didn't want to piss off Draymond and have him do her dirty like he had Radcliff. The idea of giving herself to strange men made her want to puke. But she wasn't foolish enough to deny the pimp what he wanted. Besides, if she was to leave him, exactly where would she go? She didn't have any family or friends to run to, so, unfortunately, she had to play the hand she was dealt.

Draymond gripped Constance's thigh as he watched her vacuum one of the lines up her nostril. She whipped her head back like she'd been punched in the face, blinking her eyes. Her eyes were red webbed and glassy. She had white shit caked around her nasal passages. Her nose twitched as she was about to sneeze. Draymond warned her to fight it off.

Otherwise, she'd lose the full effect of her high, and even worse, waste his product. Constance managed to keep from sneezing. She looked around lazily and felt awesome. The heroin had her nice, real nice. She suddenly didn't care about shit, especially how her father played her and her current situation. She felt as free as a bird soaring fifty feet in the sky. Little mama was just as high, too and she didn't want to come down.

"Here you go, daddy." Cherry came back with a glass loaded with ice cubes and whiskey.

Draymond took it from her and paid close attention to Constance. A smile emerged on his face as he watched her trip off her high. He just loved introducing his bitchez to that Boy and watching them get loaded. He led them all to believe he was giving it to them to help loosen them up, which was actually true. But he was also using it to get them hooked, so he'd be able to control them. He was a puppet master and his whores were his puppets.

"You like that, lil' mama? It's got chu feeling right, right?" he questioned her. Constance nodded with a goofy-ass look on her face. He passed her the glass of dark liquor. "Gon' getcha beak wet, lil' mama, it'll increase your experience." Draymond watched Constance closely as she took a sip from the glass. She gagged and coughed, making an ugly face. The alcohol was strong as fuck. She pounded her chest with her fist and tried to gather herself. "Gon' and down the rest of it, baby." Constance did like he asked, drinking down what was left inside her glass. He took the glass and set it aside before offering her another line of heroin. She tooted it up her nose and relished in the euphoria presented to her.

"Daddy, can I have a taste, too?" Cherry asked as she massaged his shoulders. Her eyes were focused on the line of nose candy left on the plate and she couldn't wait to partake in it.

"Gon' head. You did good tonight, bitch. Daddy is really proud of you," Draymond said as he took the rolled dollar bill from Constance and passed it to her.

Cherry leaned over into the plate to snort up a line and her hair draped over. Constance gathered her hair into a ponytail and held it while she did her thing. Draymond turned Constance's chin to him and slip his tongue inside of her mouth. He kissed her deeply and noticed she didn't know how so he showed her. While Constance practiced on him, Cherry used the twenty-five-cents razor on the plate to make a couple of more lines. She tooted one of them up and brought her head back up, wiping her nose with her fingers. Her eyes were wet, and she was high as a kite.

"Now, that was much, much better," Draymond complimented Constance on her kissing skills. She smiled. He scooped a small pile of heroin into his long pinky nail and brought it to her nose. She tooted that shit up her nose like a champ. He could tell the alcohol and the Boy had loosened her up.

There was a knock at the door. Draymond already knew it was the niggaz he'd called over, so he sent Cherry's ass to open the door. As soon as she opened the door, ten cats filed in over the threshold, two of which were taking swigs of Coronas. The alpha of the pack smacked Cherry on her ass as she shut and locked the door. She cracked a smirk and looked back at him.

"Keep your hands off the merchandise, sweetie. Less you plan to buy," Cherry told him sternly.

"Shiiiiid, I love playing in the snow," Alfonzo claimed as he pulled out a wad of dead faces and waved them at her. He was a square-head nigga that rocked a baldy and a thin goatee. He wore several gold necklaces, a white T-shirt, and a leather jacket that was entirely too big.

"Well, I love a man that knows just how to get a party started." Cherry capped as she walked past him and rubbed on his protruding belly.

Draymond had hit up his cousin, Alfonso, and his boys to come over. They were a squad of ten trick-ass niggaz and they lived by that lame-ass nigga phrase, It ain't tricking if you got it. Alfonso and his boys always spent good money with Draymond. So, every now and then he'd throw them a piece of pussy for free. He'd usually let them smash a ho of their choosing, but this time he was going to let them get a crack at Constance. This way he'd be killing two birds with one stone. You know, let them thirst bucket niggaz smash and break his new girl in at the same time.

Alfonso's attention was diverted to the kitchen where Nelly's Hot In Here was blaring from one of his homeboy's cell phones. Constance's lil' ass was dancing with two of his boys seductively *while everyone else cheered them on. Draymond stood watching the show with his arm hung around Cherry's neck. He was sipping on a glass of something dark while she held a plate to her nose, tooting up a white substance. Alfonso's boys had fists full of money of all denominations and they were making it rain on Constance. Draymond whispered something to Cherry. Alfonso figured it was about her getting out there and popping her pussy along with Constance. This was because she sat the plate of powder on the counter and stripped to her bra and panties. She danced her way over to his boys and started dancing sensually with two of them herself. Hoots, hollers, cheers, and whistles filled the kitchen. As the dollars were being thrown, Draymond broke out with big ass bottles of alcohol. He had everything you could name. He started filling up see-through plastic cups and passing them out. Next, he busted out with a red ceramic sugar bowl of cocaine and another red bowl filled with pretty green weed nuggets. The next thing he came out with was rolling papers of every kind.*

Alfonso joined in on all the fun and started dancing with the girls, too. Draymond kept the alcohol and drugs flowing. Everybody got shitfaced. About an hour passed before the rest of Draymond's stable of bitchez arrived from a bachelor party they were working. After they broke him off with the gwap they'd made that night, they all freshened up and joined the festivities. The next thing Draymond knew a big ass orgy was taking place inside one of the many bedrooms in his crib. There was a whole lot of sucking, fucking, and nut shooting going down. Niggaz and bitchez were sweaty and stinking by the time everything was over.

By the time the girls woke up the next morning, Alfonso and his boys were long gone. When they came out of their bedrooms, they found Draymond sitting on the living room couch. He was counting money, and there were five different stacks lined up before him on the coffee table. Alfonso and his boys had such a good time they decided to pay him for his generous hospitality. Not only that, those niggaz tipped him. That was one thing he loved about tricks they didn't mind breaking bread. Hell, he didn't mind taking it for that matter.

All the girls were waiting for their chance to hop in the shower while Draymond was counting grips. He took the blunt that was wedged between his fingers and took a few pulls from it. He blew out clouds of smoke before snuffing out the blunt's ember tip inside of the ashtray. He then went back to counting that gwap.

Constance walked awkwardly inside the living room. She was wearing a wool robe over the bra and panties one of the girls had given her. Draymond had just finished counting the bills he had in his hands when he noticed her gap and the funny way she was walking. She sat beside him and leaned her head against his shoulders, wincing. The drugs and alcohol had finally worn off and just like the rest of the girls her entire body was aching. Alfonso and his boys had fucked them in every hole they could think of. When they got up that morning they were covered in dry semen. Some even had condoms stuck to their ass and thigh. Being that she was a virgin, Constance felt the worse out of all of them. Her twat was on fire from them grown-ass men fucking her. Not to mention, her butthole felt like it had been stretched out. Before she hopped in the shower, she took a shit and didn't even feel the dookie coming out.

"What's up witchu, lil' mama?" Draymond asked as he started rearranging and counting more bread.

"Daddy, you think I can have a lil' something to pick me up? I'm aching all over from last night." Constance looked up at him with pleading eyes and a quivering bottom lip. She looked like a sad-ass puppy.

"I can't front, lil' mama, with the way I heard you performed last night, you've earned it." Draymond tapped his cheek signaling for her to give him a kiss.

Once she did, he ducked off into his bedroom and returned with a small bag of dope. He tossed it to her, and she wasted no time ripping it open. He watched as she quickly dumped some on her fist and tooted it up her nose. She threw her head back with her eyelids shut and a smile gracing her face. She looked like she was in heaven. Again, she dipped her head low and snorted up some more of the Boy. A grinning Draymond combed his fingers through her locs as he looked at her.

Man, my lil' baby is built for this shit. Bitch took to the game so quick. To think she wasn't even down with me at first. Now, look at her! A lil' more grooming and tuning she gon' be my top bitch one day, Draymond thought as he watched Constance continue to indulge in the nose candy.

It was safe to say she was hooked on that shit. Draymond smiled knowing for as long as he had good dope, he'd be her puppet master and she'd be his puppet.

Tranay Adams

Chapter Seven

Three years later

"Haa! Haa! Haa! Haa! Haa!" Constance breathed heavily as she ran down the sidewalk. She had a warm gun in her hand and specks of blood on her shirt. Little mama had just run out of the house after popping Draymond and Cherry. Constance, Draymond, and Cherry had grown addicted to heroin. They were full-blown dopefiends now. Draymond's love for dope had royally fucked up his life. Thanks to his habit he lost his cars, jewelry, furs, all his whores, everything of value of his was gone. He didn't give a fuck either! All he cared about was getting high. If he couldn't get money for his habit the ski-mask way, he'd pimp Constance and Cherry out to get it.

Draymond's pimp hand used to be strong, but ever since he'd gotten hooked on heroin he started lacking. A lot of times his girls were left to look out for themselves while they walked The Blade. Unfortunately, a few times, a handful of them had gotten kidnapped and raped by their tricks. The girls were afraid to be out on the streets alone, so they ditched Draymond and chose another pimp. They didn't see any reason to keep risking their asses for Draymond when he was a dopefiend and would eventually spend the money on heroin. That shit didn't make any sense to them.

Without anywhere else to go, Constance and Cherry decided to stay with Draymond. They didn't sell pussy for him, but they did for themselves, to support their addiction. The girls came up with an agreement to kick him a little something for rent, utilities, and food. Everything was straight until Cherry caught The Monster (AIDS) and couldn't hustle trim to pay her share or get high. She was left depending on Draymond and he was left depending on Constance.

That night Draymond and Cherry were dope sick. They'd fell terribly ill and started puking everywhere. The only one that had any dope left was Constance and she wasn't sharing. Fed up, Draymond drew his gun to rob Constance. He got distracted by

Cherry constantly throwing up, which left Constance enough time to spring into action. She kicked him in his nuts and made him drop his gun. Constance picked the gun back up and held him and Cherry at gunpoint. Draymond and Cherry thinking she didn't have the balls to pop something, tried to rush her. She showed them how gangsta she really was and shot both of their geeked up asses. She hit Draymond high in the chest and Cherry in her forearm.

Constance knew the cops would be on their way after the gunfire, so she got the fuck out of dodge. When she fled the house, she could hear the police car sirens in the distance racing to her location. The red and blue flashing lights of the police cars shone on Constance as she ran. She ducked inside the alley and used her jacket's sleeve, to wipe her fingerprints off the gun. Grabbing the gun by its handle, she upward and flung it like a boomerang. The gun spun around fast as it made its way toward the roof of a closed nail salon. Once Constance heard it hit the surface and slide, Constance knew it made it up there. Suddenly, she was bathed in blinding headlights. She looked over her shoulder with narrowed eyelids and a hand above her brows. She couldn't make out who it was behind the wheel, so she figured whoever was in it represented danger.

Constance took off running with a van following her. She lost her equilibrium a couple of times from running before she eventually tripped and fell. She tried to get up and realized she'd sprained her ankle. Right then, the front passenger door of the van opened and a bald head, muscle-bound nigga emerged. Constance couldn't make out who he was through the blinding orbs of the van. All she could see was his silhouette, but soon she was able to see him entirely. He was a tall, white police officer that looked like he wanted all the smoke. The big mothafucka didn't look friendly at all, and he gave Constance the creeps.

Desperate, Constance scanned the alley for something she could protect herself with. Locating a 2 X 4 sticking up from a pile of black garbage bags, Constance hobbled up on her feet and hobbled over to get it. As soon as she pulled out the 2 X 4, the bald head cop upped his holstered handgun.

"Bitch, I've gotta marksman's aim, so, if you don't drop that board, I'ma drop your ass. Do you understand me?" The hulking man spoke with a Russian accent, as he aimed his gun at Constance's forehead. He was a second from pulling the trigger and splattering her brain fragments on the wall.

Constance, sweating from running, took a deep breath before slinging the 2 X 4 aside. She then threw her hands up in surrender. Using his gun, the cop motioned for her to turn her back to him while he applied white plastic zip ties. She followed his directions and he fastened the zip tie around her wrist. He then holstered his gun and escorted Constance to what she discovered was a police van. Her brows furrowed figuring she'd gotten caught up in a sweep, but that wasn't exactly the situation here.

The Russian cop popped open the backdoors of the police van. He grabbed Constance's arm and helped her climb inside. She sat down and took a look at all of the women held up inside with her. That's when she realized that most of them, she knew from off the Ho Stroll. They were all whores and most were addicted to some sort of drug.

"Constance, is that chu?" A bony dark-skinned girl inquired. She rocked a weave that looked too heavy for her petite body. She was wearing a white tank top and tight-fitting black jeans. Little mama went by the name Frankie. She was one of the prostitutes that jumped ship on Draymond when he started fucking with that Boy tough.

"Frankie?" Constance tried to peer through the darkened van at her. She could partially make out her facial features, but she wasn't sure if it was her or not.

"Yeah, it's me, girl. You still with—" Frankie was cut short by the angry, pink-faced Russian.

"You whores quiet down in there for I take this can of mace." The Russian cop pulled a can of mace from the black leather holster on his belt. He held it up for all the women to see. "And burn your fucking eyeballs out of your skull!" he threatened with flaring nostrils and clenched teeth. He hoped the women defied

him so he could blast them in the face with the fiery hot liquid. *"That's what the fuck I thought."* He holstered the can of mace, slammed the double doors shut, and locked them.

Once the Russian hopped into the front passenger seat and the van drove off, the girls started back talking in hushed tones. Constance found out that Frankie, unlike the other girls, had gone rogue. In other words, the bitch was working for herself in the streets. She'd gotten busted by an undercover cop out on Figueroa. That's how she ended up in her current situation.

Constance and Frankie continued to chop it up. They caught up with the happenings in one another's lives. Constance was more than happy to talk to her homegirl. They were like sisters when she was under Draymond's thumb. They had even gotten one another's name inked on their arm. On top of that, Constance needed to converse in order to keep her mind off her fate. She knew she'd been snatched up for the shooting back at Draymond's crib. The only thing she didn't know was whether Twelve was going to nail her to the cross for two attempted murders or a double homicide. The charges depended on whether Cherry and Draymond's punk asses were still alive. Should either of the two charges stick, she knew she wouldn't see the streets for a long ass time. That was, unless, she could get a bad-ass attorney that could come up with her a decent defense. Constance decided to worry about that kind of stuff later, though. Right now, she was getting reacquainted with her bitch.

All the girls had fallen asleep or nodding off when the police van finally reached its destination. They didn't even hear the double doors of the van being unlocked. When the Russian cop pulled the doors open, a ray of light shone on all their faces, but they still didn't wake up. The Russian cop, who was soon joined by another one, placed a megaphone near his thin lips.

"Alright, you whores! I want your asses up and off this van in a single file line! Let's go, let's go! Move it, move it, move it!" The Russian cop's voice boomed loud and clear.

The heightened volume of his voice startled all the girls out of their sleep. They looked around wide-eyed like they didn't know *what the fuck was going on. Once the cop's words registered in their foggy brains, they jumped to their feet and hurried out the van. As soon as they stepped out of the back of the transporting vehicle, they were overwhelmed by the warm rays of the sun. Their faces scrunched up and they looked away to avoid its intense light.*

Standing in line, the girls looked around to find themselves inside of a compound, loaded with parked cars. The one that stood out the most was a milk-white 2011 Chrysler 300C with the license plate: Momma. The vehicle was sitting on twenty-inch tires and had pitch-black tinted windows. On either side of it were small Russian flags which made the whip look real presidential. Constance didn't know who the car belonged to, but she figured whoever was in charge owned it.

Hearing a tearing sound, the girls looked over their shoulders, to see the Russian cop that drove the van pulling off the huge Los Angeles Police sticker from the side of the vehicle. He balled the sticker up and tossed it into a nearby trashcan. He then picked up the shotgun he'd leaned up against the van and hoisted it on his shoulder. The girls' faces frowned up. They'd suddenly realized that they weren't at a police station.

"Aye, man, where the fuck are we?" A scowling Frankie asked one of Russians.

When she looked to him, he was snatching off his policeman's uniform with one tug. The other Russian cop, who was the driver of the van, followed suit. They tossed their uniforms inside the van and shut the doors. They were now wearing black fatigues and matching black caps, all of which had security stitched on them. The girls gasped when the men that they were tricked to believe were cops reveal them true selves. They all started to worry now. They didn't know what they'd allowed themselves to get put in.

"You mothafuckaz ain't cops!" One of the girls stated the obvious.

"What the fuck's going on here?" A second girl demanded to know.

"Yo, bro, where are we, and who the fuck are you people?" Frankie asked more heatedly this time around.

One of the Russian's walked up to her and slammed the stock of his shotgun into her stomach. Her eyes bulged and she doubled over, harping and coughing. The son of a bitch had knocked the wind out of her. He followed up by whacking her across the back of her skull with the butt of the shotgun. Teary-eyed, Frankie crashed to the ground harping and coughing.

The Russian scowled and spat on the ground near Frankie. "Any more of you whores got any questions?" The girls were as silent as the grave. They didn't want to get what Frankie had gotten, or even worse.

The Russian that had assaulted Frankie walked past Constance and she mad dogged him. She wanted to beat his ass, but she couldn't do anything with her wrists restrained. She had to suck up her anger and push on through.

The Russian that walked past Constance took the front of the line while the other took the back. The one at the head of them motioned for them to follow him. They did. As the girl walked forward, they looked up at a huge complex that reminded all of them of the Men's Central Jail. It had about ten floors and there were guards on each one of them. They were all dressed like the Russians that had brought her and the Russian's there. They were also packing shotguns like them as well.

As they approached the double glass doors of the complex, the two-armed guards standing before them opened it. The girls were led inside over the threshold where they were to go through a metal detector. Another guard sat behind a desk behind a keyboard and monitor that displayed everything the girls had on them. There was a total of ten girls in all, and the metal detector blared when each one that went through it. One of the Russians that came with girls in the van pulled out a box-cutter and sliced off all their zip-ties.

He instructed the girls to empty their pockets, strip down naked, and place all their articles of clothing inside an industrial-sized hamper he provided. The girls did like he said, and he led them through another metal detector, which was located at the door of another room. The girls filed through this metal detector, but its alarm didn't blare this time.

The other Russian brought up the single-file line of the girls as they made their way inside of the room. Just like when niggaz hit the county jail, they were made to show every opening, crease, crack, and crevasse of their bodies. They were even made to squat and cough. Some of the girls had been out on the streets all day and night working. So, the room they were in smelled like booty, sweat, musk, and piss. When the probing was over, the girls were led to the shower room where they showered. They dried off and were provided hospital gowns and crocs.

They were given clean bras and panties. Some of the bras had a wire sticking out of them, and most of the panties had vaginal discharge stains in them. Once the girls were in their underwear, they were all given a hospital gown and one pair of crocs. They were then taken to the eighth floor. They left the elevator and entered a dorm.

The dorm was lined up with bunk beds that were made up of military-style. Each set of bunk beds sat beside its own two lockers, to accommodate the girls. There were thirty-inch flat-screen televisions mounted on each wall, and there was a huge bathroom. It had rows of toilets with dividers on each side, a row of sinks, and a shower room off to the side, by itself.

There was a wide-open path at the center of the eighth floor, where the girls were made to line up. Ahead of them, there was a tall white woman who looked like she was drop-dead gorgeous in her prime. She was dressed in a ruffled collar blouse, pencil skirt, and matching jacket. Her blonde hair was pulled back in a bun, to show off her beat face, pearl earrings, and necklace. She had the most beautiful shade of jade green eyes, and her smile was enchanting. Upon meeting her you'd swear she was the nicest, sweetest person you'd ever met.

You'd be a fool to believe that. This was Momma. The wicked-est, most coldhearted bitch to have ever worn a pair of pumps. All she cared about was money and power. She didn't give a fuck who she had to use or what she had to do to get either one. Standing beside her, was a white man that was even taller than she was. He was wearing glasses, a plaid button-down shirt, and a lab coat. His shiny white name tag read: Dr. Kendrick. Next to him, was a thirty-five-year-old average looking, white woman. She was dressed in a throwback, all-white nursing uniform with the hat, stockings, and shoes to match.

Momma took in all the faces of the women before speaking, "Like it or not, you all belong to me now," she began. "You will work day and night, Monday thru Saturday with Sunday off. As for when you'll be free to leave, well, that depends on you. I expect five-hundred-thousand dollars in buy out money. Now, that may seem like a lot to you, but I deal with a very wealthy clientele. I'm talking about doctors, attorneys, judges, politicians, and so on and so forth. Once you've made my half of a million dollars, you'll be free to walk." Momma was lying through her fucking teeth.

She had no plans of releasing any of the girls she'd kidnapped. She feared that they'd informed the authorities so once she was done with them—she'd kill them. Afterward, she'd sell their organs on the black market and make a fortune. Prostitution and organ trafficking made her a multibillionaire. It was her bread and butter and she wasn't going to let anyone get in the way of her making her coins.

Momma went on to explain that there wasn't any escape for the girls. Not only was she connected to very powerful people, but she had a unit of men at her disposal called Hunter Killaz. Their job was to capture her girls and bring them back dead or alive—if possible. Momma assured them the punishment for trying to escape was so malevolent that they'd wish they'd been killed. She then became silent and allowed her words to soak into their brain, before continuing with what she had to say.

"Okay, today Dr. Kendrick will give you a pat smear, a full physical, give you immunization shots, and test you for STDs," Momma informed them. "Also, a tracking device will be surgically implanted behind your ear. This is for me to know where you are at all times. Should you leave outside the coverage area of where you're supposed to be, I will press a button that will make the tracking device explode, blowing your head into itty, bitty pieces."

She turned to Dr. Kendrick. "Are you ready for them now, doctor?" Dr. Kendrick nodded.

The doctor and his nurse went about the task of working on the girls. The girls that tested positive for an STD were given medications to treat it. If it was found that they had something more serious like herpes, they were taken off the floor and shot dead down in the basement. The rest of the girls went on to the final procedure, which was having the tracking device surgically implanted behind their ear.

Half of the girls had completed the procedure when it was time for Constance's friend, Frankie, to enter the doctor's office. Constance could tell by the look on her fiend's face that she wasn't up for going through the shit Momma had told them about. For as long as she'd known her, she'd been a fighter. It didn't matter how big or small a nigga or bitch was Frankie would bring drama to their asses. Lil' mama was just as tough as any nigga on the street and she didn't mind getting her hands dirty either.

Frankie went inside the doctor's off and the nurse shut the door behind her. Ten minutes later, the entire floor was startled when they heard shouting coming from the other side.

"You mothafucking white folks got me fucked up! Y'all have been pimping our black asses for four-hundred and something odd years. Now you think you finna keep doing it? No way! No-fucking-way! Today is a new day, I am not my ancestors!" Frankie's voice rang out from the doctor's office and drew everyone's attention.

The door of the office swung open, and Frankie, who held a scalpel to Dr. Kendrick's throat, led him out of the room. Everyone noticed the nurse lying stiff on the office floor behind them. Her eyes were vacant, her mouth was wide open, and her throat had been slashed, blood spurted and poured out of the slash, quickly expanding on the floor.

The rest of the girls came together collectively watching and waiting to see what would happen. The Russian guards stepped in front of Momma and formed a human-wall for her protection. They then hoisted up their AR-15s and kept them trained on

Frankie. The deadly ends of their assault rifles followed her as she made her way around the room.

"I'm getting outta here, and no one is going to stop me! You hear me? No one!" Frankie called out to anyone that would listen. She had the scalpel pressed so hard against Dr. Kendrick's neck a trickle of blood ran from it. "Drop your guns!" she demanded of the guards. When she saw that they weren't obliging her orders, she grew irate. "I said, drop your guns, or I swear before God and heaven, I'll slit this cracka's throat from ear to ear!" Frankie listened as Momma said something to the guards in Russian. In turn, they dropped their AR-15s. "Now, kick them across the floor!" Momma gave the guards the word and they did like Frankie commanded.

Frankie looked at Constance who was already looking at her. They communicated through their eyes that Constance would join her in her escape. "Connie, pick up those guns and bring 'em over here to me! We're getting outta here, mama, you and me!" Constance went to pick up the AR-15s that the guards had kicked out of their reach.

Unbeknownst to her, Dr. Kendrick communicated with the guards with a look. The guards slightly nodded their understanding. Taking Frankie by surprise, Dr. Kendrick's elbowed her in the side with all his might. The swift blow caused her to howl in pain and drop the scalpel. Frankie bent at the waist holding her aching ribs and the good doctor shoved her up against the wall. He dove out of the way as the guards came from around their backs with guns. Constance watched in horror as the guards brought their guns up, aimed, and spat fire. Bullets zipped through Frankie's body and spray painted her blood against the wall behind her. She collapsed to the floor, eyes wide, bloody mouth open, she was dead!

"Noooooooo!" Constance hollered aloud in emotional pain as tears flooded her cheeks.

She tried to run over to a lifeless Frankie, but the rest of the girls, who were saddened by her tragic death, held her at bay. Constance hollered and hollered before going limp in the girls' arms. She bowed her head, big teardrops fell from her eyes, and her body shook traumatically.

***

"They killed her, right there in front of me!" Constance broke down sobbing, tears cascading down her face. "Cut her down like she was nothing—less than nothing!" she cried out.

Fear wrapped his arms around her affectionately. He truly felt sorry for her. Her story was touching and made him teary-eyed. Rocking her back and forth in his arms, he kissed the top of her head. She told him to hold her tighter and he granted her request.

"I got chu now, ma. And I swear no one is going to hurt chu ever again," Fear swore to her. "And as far as all of them bitch-ass niggaz and them ho-ass bitchez, they're dead. You hear me? All those mothafuckaz are dead! I'm gon' get at 'em all, they gon' feel it. Rest assured." He continued to console Constance and she continued to cry.

After a while, Constance fell asleep in his arms. He picked up his Heineken from the nightstand and took swigs of it. He hadn't drunk half of it before he felt himself growing sleepy. Abruptly, sleep overcame him, and he released the beer bottle. The bottle hit the carpeted floor spilling some of its contents and rolling a short distance.

Constance stirred awake from her fake sleep. Smiling mischievously at Fear she kissed him on his lips and pulled his pajama pants below his nut sack. She kept an eye on him as she stroked his dick making it long, fat, and strong. She licked him from the line in his nut sack, up to his shaft, and outlined his bulbous head with her tongue. A bubble of transparent semen oozed out of his pee-hole and she went to work on him. Constance sucked him up while jerking him up and down. Fear moaned in his sleep and smacked his lips like he tasted something. She didn't pay him any mind as she continued to cast her spell until he was at his full potential.

Constance brought her head up from Fear's dick and wiped

her glistening mouth. She then straddled his waist, placed her hands flat on his pecs, and slowly lowered herself onto the tip of his pulsating piece. His dick poked at her taint missing her engorged pussy lips by a mere inch. She tried to come down on him again, but she missed him once again. Using her hand, she held his piece still and lowered her pink hole onto him. Constance gasped and grinned feeling Fear's girth stretch her pussy open. She started off riding him slowly and then she went faster and faster. Once she found her rhythm she went for broke. His dick felt so good that her eyes rolled to their whites and her mouth hung open. His curved piece was hitting her spot.

"Aaaah, fuck!" Constance said under her breath so she wouldn't wake him. She continued to ride him intensely occasionally glancing down at his face. He winced on and off, but she was sure he didn't know that it was her that was fucking him. What he said next confirmed that for her.

"Dammnnn, Italia, baby, you got some good pussy, shiiittt!" Fear said with his eyes shut.

The next thing she knew he was grabbing her around her waist and pumping upwards into her. His face balled up and his jaws were clenched. Still, she knew he wasn't coherent to what was transpiring. In his dream, he believed he was fucking Italia, but he was actually fucking her. Constance didn't care though. She could imagine otherwise until the day came when he was well aware of who he was smashing. For now, she was going to whip that pussy on him until she caught that nut.

"Oh, shit! I'm cumming, I'm cumming!" Constance threw her head back and rode him faster and faster.

As she reached her orgasm, she released a blissful scream but quickly slapped her hand over her mouth. She continued to work her hips on top of Fear, looking down at him smiling happily. She could tell by the way his hands gripped her waist and the expression on his face he was nearing his nut. A minute thereafter, he grunted and pumped upward into her.

She tightened her walls around him as she felt him skeet inside her womb. His warm gooey semen came out in spurts at first before shooting out in great force, painting her insides white. Constance bit down on her bottom lip and continued to ride him, milking his dick until there wasn't anything left. Once she felt his piece shrinking, her movements stopped, and she looked down at him.

A smile spread across her face as she thought; *Too bad I'm on the pill. I know our child would be beautiful. We could have a baby boy. A baby boy with the perfect combination of our features. He'd have all our strengths and none of our weaknesses.*

Fear's face returned to how it looked when he was asleep, and he released her waist. Constance leaned forward and kissed him. She laid against him and shut her eyes, imagining what it would be like to be his woman. The thought of being able to call him hers and him being able to call her his made a smile spread across her lips. Her heart swelled with all the love she had to give him and completely consumed her. So much so she couldn't stop the words that escaped her lips.

"I love you, Fear," Constance told him with her eyes still shut.

"I love you too, baby." Fear said in his sleep, believing he was speaking to Italia.

Constance basked in Lala Land a while longer before peeling her hot sticky body up from Fear's. As naked as Eve was in that garden, she crept out of the bedroom and returned with a wet washcloth. She cleaned up Fear's dick and balls. Afterward, she kissed the head of his piece and placed it back inside his pajama pants. Once she slipped her robe back on, she covered him up with the blanket on his bed, kissed him on his lips, and made her way toward the door. Constance opened the door, but before she left out, she looked back at Fear peacefully sleeping. A lovesick expression spread across her face as she held the door open and admired him openly. She blew him a kiss and disappeared through the door, closing the door gently behind her.

Constance placed her back up against the door of Fear's bedroom. She looked up at the ceiling smiling. She was smitten by the certified killa. He had her so far gone. Cupid had shot her crazy ass with his bow and arrow. Suddenly, Constance became giddy and threw her fists up, jumping up and down. Little mama was excited! She spun around in circles and danced down the hallway, singing *Jackie Wilson's To Be Loved.* Finally, she entered her bedroom and shut the door behind her for a good night's sleep.

Chapter Eight

Morning

Constance stirred awake from the delicious aroma of breakfast being cooked. She sat up in bed stretching and yawning. When she looked to her nightstand, she found items for her to take care of her hygiene, undergarments, socks, a T-shirt, and a pair of sweatpants. Constance slid out of bed, took care of her hygiene, got dressed, and headed inside the kitchen. She leaned in the doorway with her arms folded against her breasts.

A smile spread across her face as she watched Fear with his back to her. The muscles in his muscular back flexed as he stood over the stove, whipping up breakfast. He was wearing a black du-rag and sweatpants that he'd cut the legs off of. Constance admired Fear for a minute, thinking it was nothing sexier than a street nigga that knew his way around the kitchen. The thought of it made her nipples perk up and her pussy moisten.

Constance decided to sneak up on Fear and scare him. She held her hands held up as she tiptoed toward him as quietly as she could. She was quickly closing the distance between them when he suddenly swung around and pointed a black gun at her. Constance froze in her tracks and her eyes locked on a bright red dot. It traveled up her torso and unbeknownst to her, it settled on her forehead. When she finally locked eyes with Fear, he had a serious look across his face and then a smile spread across his lips. Constance smiled and lowered her hands as he lowered his gun.

"Girl, how're you gon' try to creep up on me? I studied under the best. I'm not new to this I'm true to this," Fear told her as he tucked his gun at the small of his back. He then turned the fire off from under the pans on the stovetop.

"Aye, you can't blame a girl for trying." Constance leaned over his shoulder and looked at what he'd whipped up. "Whatchu got there, handsome?"

"French toast, Denver omelet, bacon, and grits," Fear told her as he made their plates.

"Sounds good, I can't wait to dig in," Constance told him.

"Do me a favor, slim. Grab two glasses down from the cup-board and pour me a glass of apple juice. And, uh, feel free to get yourself whatever you want to drink."

"Yes, big poppa," Constance smacked him on his ass playful-ly. She followed his instructions, except she poured herself a glass of orange juice instead. She placed Fear's glass down where he was going to sit and sat down with hers. As if on cue, Fear sat her plate down before her and his down where he was going to sit.

"You wanna do the honors and say grace?" Fear asked her, lying napkins down before both of them.

"Yeah, I can fade that," Constance assured him.

"Good," Fear said. They grasped one another's hands and bowed their heads. He listened as she graced the food.

"Bless this food to our bodies, Lord, and let us hold you in our hearts. In Jesus' name, we pray, Amen," Constance finished.

"Amen," Fear said after her.

They dug into their plates.

"I've been thinking about what you said last night. You know, about wanting to pay me back?" Fear asked before taking a bite of his omelet.

"Uh-huh, I'm listening," Constance told him, taking a bite of her French toast.

"I could use a partner out here. You know, someone to watch my back while I'm in these streets," he informed her. "I'll have to train you up in the mountains for like a year. You'll hone skills that will make you a proficient killa, a lethal weapon like I am."

Constance munched down the rest of her food and wiped her mouth. She looked him square in his eyes and said, "Whatever you need me to be I'll be it. Whether it be your partner, or your—" She rubbed her foot against his crotch underneath the table. "Fuck buddy." She smiled sexily and batted her eyelashes at him.

Fear flashed her a weak smile before sliding back from her foot. He felt himself getting a hard-on and didn't want to give her the wrong idea. "Thanks, but partner will suffice. We'll split our earnings fifty, fifty straight down the middle. Deal?" He extended his hand toward her.

"Deal," Constance agreed, smiling and shaking his hand.

Constance and Fear went back to eating their breakfast. Fear hadn't noticed Constance watching him eat and thinking of how beautiful their kids would be. She smiled thinking of how wonderful married life with him would be.

***

Later That Day

Lethal was doing pushups on the floor of his cell when Bart appeared in the doorway. He could tell by the look on his face that something had him perturbed. Lethal got up on his feet and motioned Bart inside, while he wiped his sweaty face with a towel. Bart was a buff-ass, five-foot-six Chinese cat. The Chinese man rocked spiky gelled hair and a keloid scar that stretched the length of his right cheek. His tribal ink began at his bulging pecks and ended at the wrists of his big, muscular arms. At twenty-three-years-old, Bart was easily the youngest Asian in the Asian car.

"I've got to tell you something," Bart told him.

"What's up?" Lethal asked Bart as he approached him, hanging the towel around his neck.

"Your life is in danger," Bart answered regretfully.

Lethal's ears prick up, his heart thudded, and anxiety swelled his chest. He knew this day was coming, he just didn't expect it so soon. Lethal's forehead wrinkled curiously and he placed his hand on Bart's shoulder. "What're you talking about? What's going on?"

Bart filled him in on what he'd overheard the other day. Lethal realized he had more than one hitta to worry about since Gunplay threw his hat into the ring. He figured it had to be Fear who had put the battery in his back and sent him after him. Being waist deep in drama, Lethal knew he had to plot his next move—and fast. He now had two killaz coming at him, and he didn't have an inkling of who the other one was.

Lethal leaned his back against the bunks, folded one arm across his chest, and used his other hand to massage his chin. Bart could tell he was thinking about something from the look on his face. He didn't know what, but he had to let him know that whatever danger lied ahead, he was riding with him until the wheels fell off.

"Lee," Bart called for Lethal's attention, breaking his train of thought. He looked up at him. "We're riding wit' chu." He looked around to make sure no one was watching him before he brandished his shank. His face balled up hostilely and murder glinted in his eyes.

Bart Huang was an upstanding Marine who was locked up behind a very gory murder. He'd come home from a tour of duty to find his young wife in bed with another man. The last thing he remembered was shutting his bedroom door back quietly, as not to disturb his wife and her lover. From there, he'd blacked out, his mind had drawn a blank of what had occurred over the next three hours. When he finally touched bases with reality, he was handcuffed in the back of a police car, with bloodstains on his clothes and hands, facing two homicide charges. Something within Bart's mind had snapped, granting him a time of temporary insanity. He would find out later that he'd murdered his wife and her lover in cold blood.

Bart had taken a butcher's knife out of the kitchen and returned to him and his wife's bedroom. He butchered her and her lover, stabbing them a total of ninety-nine times combined. Afterward, he watched a rerun of *That 70's Show*, while enjoying an ice-cold beer and a chimichanga. Unbeknownst to him, his next-door neighbor had reported the screams of his wife and lover, as they were being brutally murdered. The police kicked down Bart's door, roughly slung him to the floor, and embraced his wrists with cold metal bracelets.

A smirk emerged on Lethal's face seeing that Bart was down to bust a move with him. He looked to his doorway and the rest of the Asians had assembled behind Bart. He didn't know it, but the younger man had told them Lethal needed their help. The Asians' numbers were small within the jail, and they always hung together which strengthened their bond. Like all cars on lock, if you had a problem with one of them, you had a problem with all of them.

A shaved head Asian cat with a dead, cloudy eye, stepped up beside Bart. He stood five-foot-eight and had a scrawny physique, which made his jail uniform extra baggy on him. But what he lacked in size, he more than made up with heart. "Like Bart said, Lee, 'we're riding wit' chu."

"My brothers, y'all really 'bout to ride out for your comrade, I appreciate that." Lethal looked over his small army, tapping his fist against his chest. "Love y'all for it, too. But I can't let y'all get wet in this shitstorm. I gotta handle this shit myself."

"Man, fuck that, Lee, we got cho back. They see you then they've gotta see all of us," Tao said. He was the Asian nigga with the dead eye. When he spoke up the other Asians agreed with him and egged Lethal on.

***

Two-Bit stood on the top tier, hunched over the guard rail, and watching the doorway of Lethal's cell. He took a mental note of all the Asians crowding his door. They may or may not prove to be a problem when it comes to time to get rid of Lethal. Either way, he wasn't tripping off them, he was backed by a gang of animals that didn't mind getting bloody for a payday.

Make every day count, homeboy. Cause your time will be coming to an end shortly.

***

"If y'all bring it to those guys with me, you'll be slaughtered like fucking pigs!" Lethal assured them. "We're totally outnumbered in here. Our car is even smaller than the woods. If we were to move on the blacks it would be a suicide mission."

"But—" Bart started but Lethal cut him off.

"No, buts, Bart, I got this!" Lethal scowled as he told him. He then drew a shank from its secret hiding place—*snikttt*! "I'm not gon' let these fools bring the war to me, I'ma bring it to them!" Lethal swore as he pushed his way through the Asian's standing in his doorway, clearing a path. He knew exactly who the fool was that wanted him dead from the description that Bart had given him. He'd heard his name around quite frequently. He went by the name, Gunplay and had a fierce reputation for putting in work in and out of the streets. Although Gunplay was a killa, Lethal reasoned he wasn't a killa of his caliber. He was more of a trigger-happy gangbanger who'd learned the art of murder through trial and error. Whereas Lethal on the other hand was a professionally trained hit-man—Gustavo made sure of that. The kingpin wanted the deadliest killa at his disposal, so he paid top dollar to ensure that his chief enforcer was exactly that.

Lethal left out of his cell, leaving the Asians of his car exchanging confused glances. He concealed his shank as best as he could, as he walked across the floor, spotting Gunplay. The young nigga was sitting at a metal table surrounded by other crips playing dominoes, talking shit, and sharing laughs. Lethal's eyes zeroed in on the thick vein on the side of Gunplay's neck. He recalled this area of the neck being where the Carotid Artery and Jugular was located. He knew if he was to strike Gunplay there, he'd bleed profusely, and die in five to fifteen seconds—tops.

Fuck it! It's do or die now! I'm looking at the needle anyway for laying all those pigs down. What's another body gon' hurt? Lethal thought, as he got into killa mode. That artery in Gunplay's neck was calling out to him. It was like he could hear Gunplay's heart beating as the vein throbbed in his neck. Shit was crazy to him, but it was about to get a lot crazier for Gunplay once he poked his ass up.

Lethal's face was balled up angrily and his teeth were clenched, causing his jaws to pulsate. He was so engrossed with thoughts of killing Gunplay that he hadn't noticed an African American convict heading his way. Their shoulder collided and the convict almost fell from the force of the impact. He turned around and shoved Lethal, mad dogging him.

"Say, bruh, watch where the fuck you going? What, you can't see through them tight-ass eyes?" The African American convict looked him up and down. He was tall and lanky, towering over the much shorter Lethal at six-foot-two.

Lethal was shocked when he was shoved; he looked around and saw all eyes on him. Watching and waiting to see what he was going to do next. His element of surprise was gone now, too. Gunplay was holding his dominoes in his hands and keeping a watchful eye on him, like everyone else. When Lethal focused his attention back on the convict that had shoved him, he shoved him again and he nearly fell to the floor. Lethal's face balled up angrily again, with a snarl, he poked out the African American convict's eyes.

"Aaaaaaahhh!" The African American convict screamed as blood spilled from his punctured pupils and down his cheeks.

Lethal grabbed him by the front of his uniform and pulled him down to his size. The shank he held in his hand moved as swift as an attacking cobra, striking him in the chest over and over again. Dots of blood gathered quickly on Lethal's face as he narrowed his eyes into slits, to stop blood from getting into them.

"Aaaahhhh, aaahhhh, aaaahhh!" The African American screamed over and over again, blood spilling from over his bottom lip. His eyes crossed as he was feeling woozy from the loss of blood.

The African American convicts drew jail fashioned shanks and rushed to their comrade's aid. Seeing the brothers getting involved, the Asians drew their shanks as well. Everyone collided in one big ass rumble! The screams and hollers of men filled the air, as sharp metal was drove in and out of warm bodies and blood was flying everywhere. The alarm of the facility blared. The sounds of booted feet resonated in a stampede, as the riot squad came charging in with their shields, nightsticks, and tear gas.

The tear gas partially filled the room with fog blinding most of the convicts and giving them chest pains. Some of them gagged and coughed while others scrapped with the riot squad. They stabbed the squad members in the exposed parts of their bodies and some of the convicts even managed to take their shields from them. One of those convicts was Two-Bit. He had a wet shirt tied around his nose and mouth, the shield, and the length of metal he'd sharpened in his cell. He was blocking the attacks of the opposition and rewarding them with stabs to their chest and neck. Two-Bit looked like one of the Spartans from the 300 Movie as he strategically moved about with his shield and shank.

"Aaaaahhhh!" one of the convict's screamed in horror, having been stabbed in the face by Two-Bit.

"Gaaaaaahhh!" a second convict screamed in excruciation in the chest and neck. Two-Bit kicked him in his torso and sent him flying backward. Afterward, he continued his mission through the crowd to kill Lethal, so he could collect that bag.

Lethal was so busy defending himself, he hadn't notice Gunplay working his way through the battlefield toward him. He was armed with a shield and shank, too. He also was rocking a shirt over his nose and mouth to protect him from the teargas. He knocked some of the convicts out of his way with his shield, while he stabbed others. Gunplay's seven-inch steel shank went through flesh, muscle, and cartilage drawing blood and screams of agony from the opposition. He'd set his sights on Tao who was creeping up on a brother to do some severe damage to him. Dots of blood were scattered over Tao's face, neck, and the upper half of his uniform. He was so caught up in the attack he was about to launch, he neglected to watch his back, which would prove to be a mistake on his end.

Lethal stabbed one brother in the throat and his blood sprayed out of his neck. The brother's eyes bulged, and his mouth hung open, as he smacked his hand over his wound. Lethal kicked him in the chest and he flipped over a dead body lying on the floor. Whipping around, Lethal kicked a second brother across the face and flipped a third one over his shoulder that charged at him. The third brother hit the floor with a thud, and he stomped on his throat, making him howl in agony. By this time, the room was filling up with smoke and making it harder for Lethal to see through the fog. He narrowed his eyelids and coughed trying to make out who were his allies and who were his enemies. Something suddenly stole his attention, making him peer through the teargas's fog.

Oh, shit, Tao! "Taoooo!" Lethal called out to his comrade, seeing Gunplay creeping up behind him.

Tao had just stabbed an African American convict in the side of his head, leaving his ice pick like shank poking out the side of it. The African American convict hollered, as he dropped to the floor, trying to pull the shank out of his skull.

Hearing someone calling out to him, Tao looked up to see Lethal shouting to him in what appeared to be slow motion. He couldn't make out exactly what he was saying, but he knew to turn around when he saw him pointing behind him. Tao whipped around with his second shank ready to add another body to his notch count. He found Gunplay coming at him full speed ahead. He went to stab him, but Gunplay blocked his attack with his shield. He then dipped to the floor and swept him off his feet with his leg. Tao hit the floor so hard that his shank went flying into the air. Gunplay pressed his shield against him, pinning him against the floor, while he brutally stabbed him in his face. The savagery of the attack made Tao scream ear achingly loud. Gunplay pulled his shank out of him and flipped it over in his hand, watching him writher. He looked up in time to see Lethal hurling through the air with his foot outstretched toward him.

Bwop!

Gunplay threw up his shield and absorbed the force of Lethal's kick. He dropped his shank and staggered backward but was able to regain his footing. Lethal was on him like stink on shit, letting him have it. Enraged from seeing Tao so maliciously wounded, he rained kicks and punches against the shield. He came at Gunplay hard and fast making his shield feel every vibration from his assault. Realizing he was on the losing end of the fight Gunplay surveyed his surrounding for something he could defend himself with. He smiled devilishly when his eyes landed on a zip-gun. A zip-gun was made out of a staple gun and most of them were crafted to fire .22 caliber bullets. It was hands down the most dangerous weapon in jail and prison.

One of these fools in here musta dropped this mothafucka. Hopefully, it's still loaded, Gunplay thought.

He tossed the shield aside, ran toward the zip-gun, tucked and rolled past it. He came back up on one knee, lifting and aiming the zip-gun at Lethal.

Bart was moving through the fog swinging a razor-whip over his head and slashing the faces of his enemies with it. The poor bastards screamed and hollered as bloody slashes opened up on them. The razor-whip resembled the medieval times era's flail mace. It was made out of a length of wood with a shoestring attached to it. The shoestring was pulled through the holes of four razors and tied into a knot at its end.

"What the fuck?" Bart said aloud, seeing Gunplay lifting the zip-gun to shoot Lethal.

He charged at Lethal hoping to tackle him to the floor before the bullet caught him. Bart had leaped up on the metal tables, taking long steps across them en route to his comrade. He was halfway across the floor when he realized he wasn't going to reach Lethal in time.

Lethal stood frozen where he was staring at Gunplay with the zip-gun pointed at him. His eyes bulged and his mouth flung open. He locked eyes with Gunplay as he pulled back on the trigger knowing that this would most likely be his last day alive.

Pow!

Gunplay's face balled up painfully taking a foot to the jaw. A ripple went through his cheek and he felt a vibration in his teeth upon impact of Two-Bit's foot. Fire and smoke rushed out of the zip-gun, but the bullet went wild missing its intended target. Gunplay fell to the floor with a bloody grill and aching jaw, feeling dizzy. He strained his eyes looking through the fog but was able to lock eyes with Two-Bit.

"Homie's life belongs to me. So, either stay outta my way or become food—*Blood*!" Two-Bit threw down the shield and picked up the zip-gun, aiming it at Lethal.

Lethal had just been tackled to the floor by Bart. Bart was

grasping his hand and pulling him back up on his feet. They both were ignorant to the looming danger that Lethal was facing.

Easy money, Two-Bit thought, as he went to pull back on the trigger of the zip-gun.

"Ughhh!" Two-Bit hollered aloud, as he was struck across the back of his head.

He hit the floor unconscious revealing one of the riot squad members behind him. He was a suited and booted African American man with a double chin and a protruding gut. He had reinforcements behind him, and they all looked like they meant business.

"Piece of shit, no one else dies on my watch!" the African American man kicked Two-Bit in his side.

He was knocked out cold so he couldn't feel it, but when he woke up, he was going to be in quite a bit of pain. The big man barked commands at his underlings while waving his nightstick around. He watched as some inmates were placed in shackles while others were hauled to the infirmary. The ones that had lost their lives were covered with white sheets that were quickly absorbed by their blood.

Chapter Nine

On their way to the hospital to see Italia, Fear stopped by a flower shop and grabbed her a dozen roses in a vase. He also grabbed a *Get Well* balloon and a heart-shaped one that read *I Love You*. He then headed up to the hospital. They had to leave their guns inside the car since they had to go through the metal detector. It wasn't a big deal to Fear though. He wasn't tripping off not being strapped. He didn't believe that anyone would come for him at a hospital. There would be cops present and far too many people around. Besides, his enemies weren't looking for Italia they were looking for him. They didn't have any interest in harming her. Well, at least that's what he thought.

Fear and Constance hopped off the elevator and headed straight for Italia's room. When they opened the door, they found her laid up in bed. She was in a coma and had medical machinery hooked up to her body. All of which were making their respective noises. In fact, the only noise inside of the dimly lit room was the one coming from the machines.

"Hey, baby," Fear greeted Italia as he approached her bedside. He caressed her cheek with the back of his hand and kissed her affectionately on her forehead. "I brought you some roses and balloons I hope you like them." He smiled as he showed her the items he'd gotten her from the flower shop on the way over. After he let the balloons float up to the ceiling, he filled the vase with the roses halfway and sat it on the counter by the large window. He then approached Italia's bed again, pulling Constance along with him. They stood over her. "I brought someone along that I wanted you to meet. She's a friend of mine. Her name is Constance," Fear told Italia.

He didn't know if it were true or not, but he heard that people in a coma could still hear you. He hoped that it was a fact because if not he was looking like a god damn fool right now. Fear hadn't noticed it, but Constance rolled her eyes. She didn't know a damn thing about Italia, but that didn't stop her from disliking her. All she needed to know was that she had Fear's heart. Since she wanted it for herself that made her *her* arch-nemesis. As far as she was concerned her pretty ass was in her way. "Hi, I've heard a lot about chu. It's a pleasure to meet chu," Constance said with a fake smile that quickly vanished when Fear wasn't looking. She was putting up one hell of a front for him. Her performance was Oscar-worthy, hands down.

"You wouldn't believe how we met—" Fear said of Constance.

He then pulled up a chair to her bed and gave her the run-down. He told her what went down the night he went on that mission to rescue Ariel and how he ended up with Constance. He also told her that he'd invited Constance to stay with them until she got on her feet. That he had brought her on as his partner. How he had plans of taking her up to the mountains to train her like Master Hahn had trained him.

It tripped Constance out how Fear went on and on talking to Italia without her responding to him. He was so engrossed in his one-sided conversation with her that she was sure he'd forgotten she was there. He wasn't paying any attention to her at all. That really pissed her off. She wanted to bring it up to him but didn't want to sound like a jealous girlfriend.

She knew he'd think she was crazy because he wasn't even her man. Hell, they hadn't even fucked. So, she didn't even have any business being all in her feelings and shit. That would give her a bad look. It would probably turn him off altogether, and that was the last thing she wanted to do. If anything, she wanted him to be madly in love with her. Like she knew he was madly in love with Italia. The only way that was going to happen was if Italia was gone. Not just out of his life, but dead.

Fear's face balled up and he looked down at his grumbling stomach, holding it. Constance asked, "What was wrong?"

He responded, "I gotta take a shit! I'll be right back!" He pulled out his cell phone so he could play video games on it while he sat on the toilet.

In a flash, he was darting across the threshold of the bathroom and shutting the door behind him. Once Constance heard the door lock behind him, she walked around Italia's bed slowly, keeping her envious eyes glued to her. She couldn't believe how beautiful she was. Her looks combined with all the great things she'd heard about her made her irresistible. So, she could see how Fear could fall in love with her. Truthfully, she couldn't blame him. Still, if she was going to be the number one lady in Fear's life, Italia would have to go. There weren't any ifs, ands, or buts about it. Her death would definitely break the assassin's heart. But that's okay because he'd have her there to help mend the broken pieces together and find a new love—within her.

As Constance circled Italia's bed, she came upon the machinery she was hooked up to. She kept her eyes on the comatose woman as she glided her finger over the top of the machinery. She stopped at the heart monitor and shut it off. Now, the only machine making any noise was the ventilator. As a matter of fact, the only thing that could be heard besides that was the hospital staff out in the hallway. As well as the sounds of other medical machinery located in nearby rooms.

Constance leaned down and kissed Italia gently on the cheek. It was *The Kiss of Death*! She then grasped the crinkly hose of the ventilator with both hands and bent it. This restricted the oxygen that was being pumped inside of Italia's lungs. Constance stared down into Italia's face with hatred written on her face and her jaws clenched tight. She wanted her to die so bad her clit was hard. For a couple of minutes, Italia wasn't moving. Then suddenly her eyelids started to twitch, and her lips began to quiver. Both of her hands clawed at the sheets and created wrinkles in them. She twiddled her toes. Her forehead creased with lines as she struggled to breathe.

Seeing Italia fighting for her life excited Constance. A sinister smile spread across her face and she bent the hose further. This caused Italia to move slightly faster than she was before. Abruptly there was a loud flush that drew Constance's attention. "Fuck!" Constance said under her breath. She knew Fear would be coming out of the bathroom soon. So, she needed Italia to hurry up and die already. "Will you give it up and die already? You're making this shit harder than it has to be," Constance said through clenched teeth in Italia's ear.

She then smacked her across the face viciously and left a red hand impression behind. Keeping the ventilator hose bent, she stood upright and watched the bathroom door. She could hear Fear the faucet water running inside of the sink, so she knew he was on his way out. Her eyes darted over to Italia and her movements were starting to slow. Hell, she was started to turn pale in the face for the matter.

That's it, bitch! Just let go! This shit is almost over! Constance thought as her eyes darted back and forth between the bathroom door and Italia's face.

Hearing the squeak of the dials as Fear turned the water off, she cussed under her breath and stomped her foot. She knew she didn't have enough time to succeed in killing Italia now. Constance sighed with disappointment and released the ventilator hose. Once the oxygen started pumping back into Italia's lungs, her body seemed relieved.

There's always next time, Constance thought as she turned the heart monitor back on. Hearing the bathroom door's lock coming undone, she hurriedly tiptoed back over to the other side of the bed where she was when Fear left to go to the bathroom. Her scandalous, trifling ass gently rubbed Italia's arm and started telling Italia about how lucky she was to have a guy like Fear.

Fear came out of the bathroom drying his hands on the paper towels from the dispenser. Once he'd finished with the towels, he balled them up and tossed them into the wastebasket. A smirk was fixed on his face seeing Constance talking to Italia. He thought it was sweet seeing her take to her like she was her homegirl or something.

"Well, I see the two of you are getting well acquainted," Fear said as he looked over Constance's shoulder at Italia.

"Yeah, I wish she could say something back, though," Constance told him.

"Me too, I know her, so I try to imagine what she'd say back after I told her something," he confessed.

Fear and Constance kicked it with Italia for one more hour. He kissed her goodbye and told her nurse to be sure to call him if her condition changed for the better. The nurse assured him that she would, and he and Constance left. They just stepped off the elevator onto the parking lot ground floor when he got a call for another job. The conversation was short and sweet. Plus, nothing incriminating was said between the two parties. Fear disconnected the call and headed to pick up his first half of the gwap for the hit.

***

The night was still young when Yogi lumbered his three-hundred-and-fifty-pound body out of his apartment and adjusted his gun on his waistline. He was in the middle of getting rode like a mechanical bull by his hood rat of the week when he'd gotten a call from his homeboy saying he needed a half of a brick. It was *Money Over Bitchez* for Yogi so he pushed little mama off him, jumped out of bed, and threw on something real quick. His attire was a navy-blue NY fitted cap, a navy-blue Dickie button-down shirt, and matching Dickie shorts. The first button of his shirt was fastened so it would stay open to show the white T-shirt he wore underneath it. He was rocking his shit like the Cholos in East Los Angeles.

As Yogi made his way across the outside hallway, he looked at himself in the window of the neighboring apartment unit. He had diamond earrings in his ears that were so big they looked like they were too heavy for his earlobes. An icy gold Cuban Link chain hung against his protruding belly and held on to a gold piece. The gold piece was a stack of four kilos of cocaine. In front of the four keys, in diamonds, was *Brick Boyz*.

As Yogi stood in the window looking at himself, he smiled and boasted his mouth full of gold slugs. He then balled his meaty fists and threw up his tattooed arms. He showed off the icy gold Presidential Rolex on his left wrist and the two Cuban Link bracelets on his right wrist. Next, he held up both of his pinky fingers. They both had two big ass icy gold rings on them. The big nigga was feeling himself and you couldn't blame him. He had bossed up!

Yogi ran with a crew of killaz who got theirs the ski-mask way. It was nothing for them to kidnap a kingpin for some cheddar, or kick a dope boyz crack house door in. They didn't give a fuck who you were if you had it, then they were coming after your ass. Yogi had met up with this ese out of Watts to cop fifty bricks of blow from him. When dude showed up, he and his homeboys found themselves ambushed. Yogi and his goons pulled out those choppaz on them and made them come up off the coke. It was their biggest score yet. All the homies saw a nice bag off the lick!

Shit, at first, Yogi's jack boy crew didn't have a name but seeing how they came up on all of those bricks. They decided that they should roll with the name *Brick Boyz* since they had so many of them. In fact, everybody in the crew went and got their clique's name inked on them and copped matching iced out chains. Now with all the fly-ass whips they were rolling and the flashy jewels they were rocking, they looked more like superstar rappers than the grimy street niggaz they truly were.

Yogi snatched off his fitted cap and rubbed his jeweled hand across his swirling waves. He slapped the cap back on his head and made his way down the stairs. A grin curled the corner of his mouth as he thought about all the sexual positions he was going to have Tameka's hot-ass in once he made it back to the crib. He loved ratchet bitchez. He couldn't get enough of them. The best thing about them was that you didn't have to give them much to take them down. A little liquor, some weed, and their choice of fast food and they were willing to get it cracking.

Once Yogi reached the landing, he came across four thug ass niggaz. The ensemble was a part of his Brick Boyz jack clique. He exchanged pleasantries with them and dapped them up. They were all decked out in designers and wearing identical Brick Boyz chains. Two of them were standing upright with stacks of blue faces clutched in their hands while the other two were on their bending knees. One of the two members on their bending knees was shaking a pair of dice in his fist. Four different piles of money was on the asphalt. There was also a bottle of Hennessy and two blue plastic cups of alcohol next to it on the ground. The two Brick Boyz that was standing upright passed a blunt between them and occasionally blew clouds of smoke into the air. Their eyes were red webbed and glassy. They were as high as a giraffe's ass.

"Where you headed, Cuz?" Jaquise asked as he glanced at Yogi and then focused his attention back on the crap game. He was a scrawny, brown-skinned nigga who wore his shoulder-length hair in cornrows. He wore a red Nike beanie and a matching red and white Nike tracksuit.

"I gotta few moves I gotta make, my nigga. Lemme hit that," Yogi said, as he extended his chubby fingers for the blunt.

His cheeks ballooned as he took a few puffs of the bleezy, causing smoke to waft around him. He passed the blunt back to Jaquise and made his way toward the black iron-door, huffing and puffing out of breath. It wasn't long before he found himself leaning up against the apartment complex's resident mailboxes, trying to catch his breath. Yogi wiped the sweat that trickled from his brow and threw his head back, taking swallows of the night's cool air.

"Goddamn, a nigga needa go onna diet." He took the liberty to wipe his perspiring face with the lower half of his shirt, which showed his protruding, hairy gut.

Afterward, he continued his beeline across the apartment grounds until he reached the black iron-door, which he made his way through.

"Haa! Haa! Haa! Haa! Haa! Haa!" Yogi sounded like a fat ass hog huffing and puffing out of breath.

He was sweating profusely by the time he made it to his Burberry Blue Chevrolet Monte Carlo with thirteen-inch chrome, Dayton, wire rims. Yogi leaned up against the hood of the ghetto famous vehicle. He wiped the beads of sweat from his forehead and tried to catch his breath. His cell phone rang, and he looked at its display. It was his homeboy, Loco, from around the way. He was looking to cop half a bird off him. He had it in a brown paper bag stashed in the front of his Dickies.

"What's up, Cuz? I'm on my way now so have yo' ass there. Nah, for real, for real, I'm headed to my ride right now. On the dead locs—" A red dot appeared on the side of his face. He could see the red light shining from a distance from the corner of his eye. Yogi turned around with a frown fixed on his face. He heard a chirp in the darkness and then something hot pierced him below his jaw.

Yogi's eyes bugged and his mouth flew open. Blood oozed from the gaping hole in his neck. He dropped his cell phone and slapped his hand over his bleeding wound, slicking his fingers wet. He made gagging sounds as blood continued to pour out of him and soil the collar of his shirt. He staggered around like Franken-stein, bumping into a parked Rav 4 truck and flopping down on his back. His mouth moved like a fish out of water while blood continued to pour out of his wound. After a while, his eyes remained open and his mouth stopped moving.

Fear emerged from the shadows wearing a black hood over his head, which only left the lower half of his face visible. He casually strolled over to his latest victim with a black Heckler & Koch MK 23 semi-automatic handgun. It was equipped with an infrared laser and had a silencer on its barrel. Fear stood over Yogi and put one in his forehead. He leveled his gun at his heart and popped two more in him. The silencer of his gun wafted with smoke as he lowered it and walked off. Once Fear was out of sight, a stray cat wandered over to Yogi's limp body and started licking his blood.

"Hello? Hello? Yogi? Yogi, are you there, Cuz?" Loco called out from the cell phone, which was lying two feet away from Yogi's rigid body.

A few seconds later, Fear zipped by Yogi's dead body on a black Ducati. The whining of the bike caused the cat to run away. The motorcycle also drew the attention of Jaquise and the rest of the Brick Boyz. When they saw Yogi lying with his blood and gray brain matter scattered on the pavement, they drew their guns and ran in his direction.

"Ah, fuck, Cuz, niggaz shot Yogi!" Jaquise called out as he

ran toward the entrance of the apartment complex, leading the pack of Brick Boyz.

Unfortunately for Yogi, the Mexican kingpin that he and the Brick Boyz jacked for that weight had dropped a bag on his head. Fear fulfilled the contract the following night, which was that night.

***

Vroooooooom!

Fear ripped up the street turning the lines in the road into blurs. He was going so fast his clothing was ruffling against the blowing wind. Two black and gray pigeons pecked at half of a stale hotdog bun, which was lying in the middle of the street, flapping their wings sporadically. Fear flew through the flapping birds, splattering them, leaving feathers floating in the air and a bloody smear on the street. Looking ahead, Fear saw police cars with their sirens wailing heading in his direction, on the opposite side of the street. The police cars sped right past him. Seeing that they weren't in pursuit of him, Fear made a left turn down a residential street, where a large moving truck was waiting for him inside an alley.

Constance stood beside the huge vehicle wearing her locs pulled back in a ponytail. She rocked a cap pulled low over her eyebrows to conceal her identity, a black Dickie jumpsuit, and a puffy jacket over it. She took pulls of a Newport and blew out clouds of smoke while tapping her booted foot impatiently. She stood with one hand behind her back gripping a handgun with a silencer on its barrel. When she saw Fear zipping down the alley toward her, she dropped the cigarette at her boot and mashed it out. Once she stashed her blower inside of her jacket, she opened the shutter of her truck and extended its ramp to the ground.

As soon as Fear drove up inside the back of the truck, Constance put the ramp back up and pulled down the shutter, locking it in place. She jumped down from the back of the truck, smacked dirt from her palms, and ran around to the driver's side of the truck. Once she was behind the wheel, she slammed the door shut and started it up. After she adjusted her side-view mirror, she made sure no one was following her, and then she drove off.

Chapter Ten

The night was cool and quiet besides the occasional car passing by bumping loud music or drivers honking their horns at the scantily clad whores walking The Blade (The Blade is where prostitutes go to sell their bodies for currency). Draymond clung to the shadows watching Cherry solicit her physical assets and sexual talents for thirsty ass niggaz looking to get their nuts off. He found himself impatient seeing as how she was only gotten the attention of one jawn in the past four hours they'd been out there. He'd became even more pissed when he discovered how much money she'd come back with. Although Draymond knew it would have been best to holler at her some place more private to avoid garnering the attention of the police, his frustration with her lack of earnings won over his logical sense. "Bitch, this all the fuck you got? Sixty funky ass dollars?" Draymond complained as he clenched three wrinkled twenty-dollar bills.

He'd graduated from snorting Heroin to shooting it since it provided a faster high. Having once been considered fairly attractive, Draymond had fallen from grace and was now a shell of his former self. He still had long hair, but his new growth was pushing his perm up from its roots. His face was slender, and his eyes were sunken in with black rings around them. To top it off, he'd developed Puffy Hand Syndrome due to his intravenous Heroin addiction. His hands were freakishly large with big bullous lesions and erythema on them. Due to the size of his hands, the dope boys from around the way nicknamed him Popeye.

"Yes, that's all the fuck I got!" Cherry told him while smoking a withering cigarette and impatiently tapping her high heel pump.

Now, some would argue that Heroin did a far worse number on her than it did Draymond. She was skinny as hell and that only made those fake ass tits of hers appear even bigger. She was wearing a black shimmery dress that hung loosely on her. Over it, she had on a fur coat that stopped at her hips. It used to be white, but it had turned a light gray from her neglecting to wash it. She and Draymond had survived being shot that night they accosted Constance. They recovered in three weeks, and when they were discharged, they got right back to chasing their high.

"These tricks ain't flocking to a bitch like they used to. Hell, you see me, I don't look as good as I did a few years ago. This motherfucking dope and this disease is killing my ass. Shit is not shaking like it used to." After adjusting the strap of her purse on her shoulder, Cherry lifted her curly red wig, which reached the middle of her back. She scratched her bald patchy scalp and dandruff caked underneath her press-on nails. She put the wig back on her head and adjusted it the way she liked it. "If you ask me, this shit is your fault."

"*My fault?* Bitch, how the fuck is this my fault?" Draymond asked, tilting his head to the side. He was wearing a royal blue suit without a shirt, so his bare, bony chest was visible.

"Cause you started hoeing yourself, fucking and sucking on niggaz wit' cho faggot-ass!" Cherry reminded him.

Draymond had lost everything he had that had value and he and Cherry were forced to live in seedy motels. Cherry wasn't bringing in as much dough as he'd like, so he started slanging dick for a living. He found out that he could charge much more for gay sex. The money was good. So, he didn't mind tricking off with men. He was fucking everything from college boys to old-ass rich, white mothafuckaz. Anyway, he fucked around and caught The Monster from one of his clients. Ended up sharing a needle with Cherry, and they've both been living on borrowed time ever since.

Draymond's face scrunched up angrily and he balled the money up and threw it at the sidewalk. Mad-dogging Cherry's shot-out-ass, he stepped so close to her she could smell the stink on his breath and see the yellowish plaque on his teeth.

"Fuck you say to me, bitch?" In a blur, his hand jumped out and latched around her throat.

He squeezed her neck so hard her eyes bulged, and her mouth flew open. Her eyes turned glassy and tears slid down her cheeks. Her face started turning a reddish-purple and a vein at the center of her forehead bulged. The cigarette dropped from between her fingers, where it was wedged and ricocheted off the sidewalk. First, Cherry tried to pry Draymond's hand from around her throat. When that didn't work, she started scratching at his face. He scrunched his face further and whipped it from left to right, to avoid her assault.

"Ho, don't chu ever, and I do mean ever, come at a nigga of my caliber like that again! Do you understand me, huh? You scraggily, Lilly white, dope fiend, pimple face, no ass having cunt! I'll snap yo puss-ass neck!"

"Fuck—ack—ack—you!" Cherry managed to get out before hawking up mucus and spitting in his face.

The gooey glob smacked him in the face and dripped off the corner of his brow. His face balled up hatefully and he wiped that nasty shit from his brow. He then, while still holding Cherry by her throat, brought his opened hand high above his shoulder. He grunted and backhand slapped the bitch with all his might. The impact from the assault split her lips bloody and sent her wig flying through the air. She landed hard on the sidewalk, wincing. She touched her lip and her fingertips came away bloody. Before she knew it, Draymond was kicking her in the temple and stomping the dog shit out of her. The pimp turned dope fiend, bit down hard on his bottom lip, and stomped his whore with all the might he could muster.

"You gon' learn to respect this pimping, bitch!" Draymond warned as he continued his brutal assault.

Draymond was so wrapped up in beating the brakes off Cherry that he neglected his surroundings. He hadn't noticed, but a man in a big hat and duster slipped out of the shadows. Reaching within the recess of his duster, the man withdrew a Mossberg 12-gauge pump-action shotgun and cocked the slide on it, *chick-chick!* The black, twenty-eight-inch barrel shotgun was now at its deadliest. The man, who was wearing a black scarf over the lower half of his face, came within five feet of Draymond before he whistled for his attention.

Draymond's eyes exploded open when he saw the lone gunman. The man hoisted up his shotgun and aimed it at Draymond, as he attempted to run. He pulled the trigger of the deadly weapon and it recoiled, as a fireball erupted from its lengthy barrel. Draymond's face contorted into agony and he clenched his jaws. The blast lifted him off his feet and left one of his shoes on the ground. Before his body could greet the sidewalk, the gunman pulled the trigger again for good measure.

Before Draymond's lifeless body collided with the ground, the gunman turned around to Cherry who was screaming in horror. He forcefully shoved the warm barrel of the shotgun inside her mouth, breaking her front teeth and bloodying her grill. Her eyes watered and tears spilled down her cheeks. She knew her death was inevitable, so she prepared to meet her fate.

"This is for Constance!" Fear, the gunman, informed Cherry.

He pulled the trigger of his shotgun and obliterated her entire skull. Her eyeball went flying in one direction while her bottom jaw flew in another. As if on cue, police car sirens filled the air and Cherry's limp body collapsed to the sidewalk.

Fear took the time to admire his handiwork before dropping the smoking shotgun beside his victims. He casually strolled away whistling, *A Hunting We Will Go*, like he hadn't just committed a double homicide. As if by magic, he vanished in the darkness. Shortly thereafter, a car was heard speeding away from the murder scene.

***

Morning

Roderick was awakened by the blaring of his digital alarm clock. He turned it off, before he sat up, stretching and yawning. He wiped the cold that accumulated at the corners of his eyes and hopped out of bed. Making his way towards his bedroom door, he dipped his hand inside his boxers and scratched his nut sack. He journeyed down the hallway and knocked on his daughters' bedroom door.

"Rise and shine, girls, time for school!" Roderick told his

fourteen-year-old identical twin daughters. "Shower, brush your teeth and get dressed. I'm gonna get breakfast prepared." He made his way toward the kitchen, ignorant of his daughters' bedroom door opening, and a nigga masked up in all black slipping out. He gently closed the door behind him, and tiptoed into the bathroom, across the hallway. Roderick's forehead wrinkled feeling another presence behind him. When he turned around and didn't see anyone, he shrugged and disappeared into the kitchen to whip him and his girls up some breakfast.

Roderick whipped up scrambled eggs, bacon, toast, and grits. He placed the girls' individual plates down at different areas of the dinner table. He poured himself a cup of hot, steaming black coffee and his kids a glass of orange juice.

"Girls, get your asses in here, so we can say grace!" Roderick called out to his daughters over his shoulder. "Come on now, it's getting late and we've gotta keep our schedule." He looked into the hallway to see if they were coming, but they weren't. "Alright, y'all are horsing around. I'm finna say my grace and eat." Roderick did just that before indulging in a fork full of eggs.

He became so engrossed in his meal that he wasn't aware of looming danger. The masked man slipped out of the bathroom, pulling a syringe from the folds of his jacket, and stealthily crept toward the kitchen.

Roderick had a mouthful of food he was munching, so he sipped his coffee to wash it down. He took another bite of eggs and that's when he felt something pinch the side of his neck. His eyes got as big as golf balls feeling an alien fluid invading his bloodstream. He lay back in his chair with a swollen cheek full of eggs. The masked man pulled out a chair, placed his syringe on the tabletop, and sat on the side of him. Roderick went to grab the fork to defend himself but discovered he couldn't move his right arm. This spooked the hell out of him. He tried to move his left arm and his legs, but they wouldn't budge either.

He was nervous now and bubbles of sweat were sliding down his forehead. Helpless, he watched the masked man sit a shopping bag on the tabletop and pull out an explosive. He sat the explosive in front of Roderick. Instantly, his eyes got bigger and his heart raced. The look of panic was evident in his eyes. He tried to reason with the masked man, but he couldn't move his mouth or his tongue.

A river of saliva with egg particles in it spilled from the corner of his mouth. He was paralyzed from head to toe. The only thing he could move was his eyes. That would be his only form of communication.

"Relax, Roderick, it's harmless without the detonator," Fear, the masked man, assured before lighting up a cigarette. Roderick seemed to calm down a little with knowledge that the explosive wouldn't go off. "You don't know me, but we have a common interest. That interest is one Ms. Bridget Volkov aka Momma."

Goddamn it! I knew this bitch would get me into some shit one day. Fuck! Roderick thought.

Fear instantly picked up the recognition in his eyes. He didn't need to confirm his love affair with Momma. He'd already done his homework on him, so he knew they fucked around. The man was close to her, so he needed him if he was going to finally exact the revenge Constance deserved.

"I want chu to place that explosive underneath Momma's car. Once you do that you are to text me using the throwaway cellular inside the shopping bag. I'll take care of the rest," Fear told him before blowing a cloud of smoke into his face. "Now, I want chu to blink once if you understand, and twice if you don't." Roderick blinked once. "Good." He tapped his cigarette and grayish-black ashes fell on the tabletop. "I also want chu to get footage of what goes on within the walls of that Hell you good ol' boys are guarding. You understand?" Roderick blinked once again.

Fear mashed out the cigarette and pulled the shopping bag closer. He removed a uniform shirt identical to the one all the guards wear at the complex. The only difference was one of the buttons on the shirt acted as a small video recording device. The footage would download to Fear's personal laptop so he'd have a copy of it. After Roderick was done with his assignment, he was to turn the evidence over to the proper authorities and become a cooperating witness.

Roderick blinked his eyes once, agreeing to the tasks presented to him.

This mothafucka must be outta his rabbit ass mind if he thinks I'm going to actually do this. Is he fucking crazy? If I can get my white ass outta this I'ma hip Bridget to this clown's plans, Roderick thought as he looked Fear square in his eyes.

He was looking scared as fuck. He was agreeing to everything he said for fear that he'd not only kill him but his girls as well.

"Good, boy." Fear walked behind Roderick and patted his shoulder. He then leaned down beside his ear. "You wanna know how I know you're gonna do everything I told you to? Because if you don't—" Fear placed a picture of Roderick's daughters on the table before him.

Their eyes were big, their mouths were gagged, and they were crying. Seeing his baby girls caused Roderick to break down sobbing, with tears drenching his cheeks.

Fear picked up a strip of crispy bacon from Roderick's plate and walked off eating it. Five more minutes went by before Roderick was able to move. He hunched over in his chair, with his hands to his face, crying his eyes out. His shoulders rocked and his body trembled. He'd gotten himself waist-deep in shit!

***

Roderick did everything Fear asked of him that day, including plant the explosive underneath Momma's car. That part of his assignment proved to be easy since the explosive clung to the bottom of her whip magnetically.

It was ten o'clock at night when Momma finally drove off the grounds of her compound. She made a left when she'd pulled into traffic and made her way down the street. Unbeknownst to her, a platinum gray 2012 Infiniti QX50, with pitch-black tinted windows had been parked across the street waiting for her. It waited until she'd gotten a good two blocks before it busted a U-turn and went after her.

"Yo, slow this mothafucka down before she gets suspicious, family, fuck wrong wit' chu?" Fear frowned at the driver from the front passenger seat.

He had the detonator in his hands. It looked like a black Game Boy except it had a long antenna and a display screen. The display showed the entire layout of the city and a blinking red dot which was moving upwards. The red dot was Bridget's car. The device also alerted Fear if he was too close to the vehicle, he was tracking to detonate the explosive. He couldn't risk being within the perimeter of the blowback because he'd likely be struck by shrapnel.

"My bad, I'm just a little nervous," Roderick admitted from the driver's seat.

His face glistened from perspiration, and he was jittery. He hated Fear for putting him in this position. He didn't want to help him kill Bridget but if he didn't he was sure he'd kill his daughters. There wasn't a woman alive that came before his kids. The way he looked at it, he could get another girlfriend, but his daughters were irreplaceable.

"Let your kids be your motivation, think about them," Fear told him, as he pointed to the picture of Roderick's twin daughters in the dashboard. "Think about how if we don't pull this off, I'm gonna make a phone call that chu don't want me to make. You got that?"

Roderick pulled up to a red traffic light. He shut his eyes and gripped the steering wheel. He took a deep breath and swallowed his spit. Once he'd calmed down a little, he peeled his eyes back open and focused on the street. The light turned green and he went through the intersection.

"You need to relax, my nigga." He looked back and forth between the windshield at the screen on the detonator. "Don't worry about nothing. I got something that's gon' get chu right." He removed the blunt he had behind his ear and passed it to Roderick.

Roderick stuck the blunt between his lips and Fear lit it for him. He took a few pulls and blew out clouds of smoke, which wafted around inside of the truck.

"You know we're not supposed to be smoking in here, right? Shit is a rental," Roderick reminded him. His voice sounded funny when he talked from holding smoke in his lungs.

"Fuck all that, put that shit in the air, homeboy. We'll worry about that later," Fear told him, eyes focused on the screen on the detonator.

They were still too close to Momma's whip. On top of that, they were around too many places with crowds of people. He wasn't trying to see anyone hurt besides the bitch that exploited Constance. If he was going to carry out her demise, he'd have to get her somewhere secluded.

Roderick continued to smoke the blunt as he drove. It wasn't long before he started to feel the full effects of the Kush and his eyes became heavier. He started to feel cool and calm. It was as if his problems had vanished and he didn't have a care in the world. He loved this feeling. He hadn't gotten faded since he was in his senior year of high school. So, he'd long forgotten the feeling it brought him. Once he'd smoked half the blunt, he mashed its ember out inside the ashtray.

Fear smiled noticing the change in Roderick's demeanor after blowing a blunt. His eyes were red webbed and glassy, and he had a goofy-ass look on his face. He was definitely under the influence.

"My nigga." Fear chuckled, as he grabbed his shoulder and slightly shook it. "You fucked up, huh? That shit feels good, don't it? It got chu right?"

Roderick smiled and nodded. He started back driving leaving Fear to focus his attention back on the detonator.

"Yo, man, she's about to jump on this freeway. It's two lights away." Roderick pointed it out to Fear.

Fear scanned the area and saw about two people out. He figured now was as good as a time as any to carry out Momma's assassination. "Fall back some, I'm finna set off the fireworks," he referred to Roderick to decrease the speed so he could activate the explosive.

Roderick eased his foot off the gas-pedal and decreased his

speed to twenty on the speedometer. The detonator let Fear know he was outside of the perimeter of the blowback. He pushed the button that triggered the explosive and a smile graced his lips. The smile quickly disappeared when Momma's car wasn't blown to kingdom come. He pressed the button again, and again, and again but nothing happened.

"What the fuck is wrong with this goddamn thing?" His face balled up angrily and he smacked the side of the detonator, repeatedly. He pressed the button again and the explosive still didn't go off. "What the fuck is up, man? Did you put the shit on there or what?" He looked at Roderick, suspiciously.

Roderick looked scared and confused. He didn't know what the fuck was going on. However, he did place the explosive beneath Momma's car, so he didn't know why her ass hadn't blown up.

"I don't know, man! I put it on her car! I swear," Roderick told him.

Fear mad dogged him and swiftly pulled out a .9mm with a silencer on its barrel. He pressed it into Roderick's cheek causing his head to bend at an angle. "Bullshit! You wanna fuck with me? Nigga, I told yo' pasty, white-ass what was gon' happen should you fuck this up, didn't I? You thought I was bluffing? Well, you gon' wish you hadn't tested my G!"

"No, no, I swear to God, man. I placed it on there, just like you told me to! I swear on the life of my daughters! Pleeeease, don't kill them! Don't kill my babies, man, please!" Roderick broke down crying, and yellowish-green snot peeked out of his left nostril.

Fear held his gun pressed against his cheek for a while before eventually removing it. He didn't know why but he believed him. "Alright, change of plans." He looked through the windshield and saw Momma getting away. "Slide up on the side of this bitch, I'ma do her myself. Hurry up before she makes it onto the freeway."

"Okay." Roderick sniffled and wiped his snotty nose with his hand.

He floored the gas pedal and the truck rocketed down the

street after Momma's Chrysler 300C. The Infiniti jerked to a stop beside the driver's side window of Momma's Chrysler. She was about to go up the freeway ramp, but the sudden appearance of the Infiniti stole her attention. Fear, wearing a red bandana over the lower half of his face, stuck his blower out of the window. He gave the driver side window of Momma's car half of his magazine. He then hopped out, popped open her door from the inside, and fed her the rest of his clip.

Bon appétit bitch!

Afterward, he fled back to the truck, reloaded his gun, and hopped back into the passenger seat. Roderick sped off with Fear's leg hanging out of the door. As soon as he slammed the door shut, the truck picked up speed and zipped up the freeway.

Fear looked into the side-view mirror at Momma's Chrysler and it unexpectedly exploded. Fear and Roderick were shocked to see the car go up in flames and black smoke. They couldn't believe their eyes. This was proof that Roderick wasn't lying when he said he placed the explosive on the car.

Fear looked at Roderick and shrugged. "Damn, thing musta malfunctioned."

Tranay Adams

Chapter Eleven

One hour later

A yellow taxi-cab pulled up in front of the police precinct. The backdoor opened, holding a manila envelope, Roderick hopped out. He was dressed in a plain white T-shirt and blue jeans. All he had on him was his driver's license, social security card, and a cell phone Fear had personally given him. He looked up at the wide, sandy-brown building as the cab drove away. He was going to turn himself in to the police and present them the manila envelope. It contained enough documentation to bring serious charges against Momma and her associates. The shit he had on them guaranteed a conviction.

Roderick's cell phone rung and he answered it. "Hello?"

"Daddy?" Tina spoke into the phone.

"Tina?" Roderick asked hopeful.

"Yes, daddy, it's me," her voice cracked with joy and sadness. She was crying, yet she happy to hear from her father again.

"Baby, where's Gina? Put Gina on the phone."

"Hold on. I'ma put it on speaker."

"Daddy, is it really you?" Gina spoke into the phone.

"Oh, God, thank you, God!" Still holding the cell phone to his ear, Roderick dropped down to the sidewalk, crying like a newborn baby. Tears flooded his cheeks and snot threatened to drip from his nose. He was extremely happy to hear from his girls again. "My babies, my babies are finally home! I love you, guys! I love you so much! You hear me?" He pulled himself up on his feet by a streetlamp. He stood there holding it while he talked to the twins.

"We love you, too, dad!" a crying Gina assured him. You could hear joy and sadness in her voice as well.

Roderick talked to the twins a little while longer. They were going to stay with his aunt and uncle on the other side of town until he sorted things out. He had cold hard evidence that would help the authorities get a conviction. So, he hoped he'd be given some sort of leniency for his cooperation in the case.

"Okay, girls, I've gotta go now. I love you," he told them.

"We love you, too."

Roderick disconnected the call, broke the throwaway cell phone in half, and deposited it into the storm drain. He then wiped his wet face with the inside of his shirt. Took a deep breath and proceeded up the steps of the precinct to face the music.

***

Fear watched the evening news on his cellular. He saw several of the staff at Momma's facility being brought out in handcuffs by the police, while a white female reporter filled the viewers in on what was going on. Afterward, there were three short interviews with the prostitutes that worked for Momma. Fear and Constance didn't finish watching the entire broadcast. Having seen enough, he plugged his cellular back up to the charger inside the car. He and Constance went on to devour their *In-N-Out* cheeseburgers and finish their chocolate milkshakes. Once they'd finished, they discarded their trash and Fear gave Constance directions to their next destination. Keeping the location in mind, she cranked up the whip and pulled off into traffic.

Having witnessed the downfall of Momma's empire on the channel five news, Fear decided it was time he gets rid of the last person on his list that wronged Constance—her father. He'd saved who he deemed the worse of her rogue's gallery for last. It really wasn't that hard for him to find where Radcliff was laying his head after so many years. He chopped it up with a couple of crack-hoes and hit the hands of a few dope fiends that finally pointed him in the right direction. Surprisingly, though Fear didn't know it, Radcliff was still laying his head in the same rundown house he and Constance were squatting in back in the day. Although Fear could have dealt with Radcliff while it was daylight, he decided to fall back and wait until night fell on the city. He'd been selling crack for years and knew that crackheads normally spent their time hustling however they could in the day, so they could spend the rest of their night getting high.

That night when he broke inside Radcliff's crib, he couldn't believe someone was living there under such conditions. If he didn't know any better, he would have sworn a family of pigs was holed up in the place instead of a grown-ass man. Not only was the house filthy, it was funky as hell. Fear had a hard time keeping down the *In-N-Out* cheese burger he'd eaten earlier that day when he smelled the odor of bodily secretions. Still, he built up the tolerance to deal with it. He was there on the account of Constance, and he meant what he'd said about guaranteeing no one would ever hurt her again, and how he'd pay those back that had.

The sun was setting when Fear took a glance at his digital watch. Five minutes later, he found himself sitting at the kitchen table in darkness, holding his Glock .19 with the silencer on its barrel. Occasionally, he'd hear squeaking somewhere within the house and feel something scurry across his booted foot. He didn't need to see in the dark to know what he was hearing, and feeling was rats. He gathered that they were hungry, but hopefully, they wouldn't have to worry about that for long. As soon as Radcliff returned he was going knock his head off and leave his rodent friends with plenty to eat.

Hearing someone at the backdoor singing an old Patti Labelle song while unlocking the lock, Fear made himself as still as a statue and gripped his gun tight. The time had finally come for him to hand down his death sentence to Radcliff. The backdoor opened and Radcliff emerged singing like he was performing before a sold-out crowd at the Garden or some shit. His singing was so god damn awful that Fear started to bust up laughing a few times. Luckily, he was able to hold frame. He was in killa-mode and needed to stay like that mentally if he was going to get the job done.

Radcliff closed and locked the backdoor behind him. He then walked over to opposite side of the kitchen and flipped on the light switch. His back was to Fear as he pulled out a small transparent baggie of crack from his pocket and recovered his beat-up, old scorched pipe from the small pocket of his raggedy jeans. He carried on singing while he went about his business of stuffing his pipe with the off-white rocks.

Radcliff stuck the pipe in between his ashy, chapped lips, and was about to fire it up until he felt someone over his shoulder. Suddenly, he stopped singing and took the crack pipe from his lips, lowering the lighter to his side. Slowly, he turned around to Fear and nearly jumped out of his own skin when he laid eyes on him. His heart thudded and he felt his palms grow sweaty. Radcliff's eyes swiftly moved back and forth between Fear and the backdoor. It was like he was pondering on whether he should make his move or not.

This old nigga looks like shit! His eyes are sunken into their sockets. He has black, baggy rings around his eyes, a receding hairline, bald spots, and a patchy scruffy, nappy gray beard. And his face—look at his fucking face. It looks like skin lying over skull. This mothafucka looks like a decaying corpse, a walking dead man. Crack is a hell of a drug, boy. I don't see how niggaz fuck with it after seeing what it's done to other people.

"Old head, I'll tell you right now. I know what you're thinking," Fear told him, straight up. "Now, you may be fast, I don't doubt that. Hell, in all my years on earth, I haven't met a crackhead that wasn't quick on his feet. But lemme put a lil' bug in yo' ear." He placed the hand on the tabletop that held his Glock, aiming it at his smoked-out-ass. "I ain't ever, and I do mean ever, met a nigga that can outrun four shots from my lil' friend here. But, hey, what the fuck do I know? You may be that nigga that's just fast enough. My question to you is—are you willing to take the risk?" Fear looked Radcliff right in his eyes. He could tell his better judgment vetoed his initial thought. "Smart man, very, very smart man."

Radcliff stared at Fear trying to place his face. He wondered how he'd wrong him during his stint as a crackhead. Did he steal crack from him? Money? Or steal something of value from him to support his habit? He kept coming up blank after blank. He figured he actually couldn't have known Fear. You see, he made it his business to remember a face. He had to distinguish whether someone was friend or foe. In the lifestyle he was in, he couldn't afford to run into a nigga he'd done dirty. He didn't want to find himself in a life or death situation.

"What—what is it that you want from me?" Radcliff asked Fear.

The gun had him shook, he couldn't seem to take his eyes off it. Fear could have easily put his blower away, but he figured fuck him! Why would he make him comfortable? He didn't deserve to be at ease when he'd done Constance foul.

"Your life," Fear said like it wasn't a big deal at all.

Radcliff's eyes doubled in size and his bottom lip quivered. His stomach twisted in knots and he felt his bladder fill. He was scared, really scared. "What I—what I do to—to you—for you— for you to want to kill me?" Radcliff asked with an emotionally shaken voice.

"Absolutely nothing, Radcliff. I can honestly admit that you've done nothing to me—personally," Fear told him straight up. "But you have wronged a very, very dear friend of mine."

Radcliff's face balled up wondering. He had a long list of people he'd done wrong. He'd be standing there all day if he decided to rattle off the names he had in mind. But he figured if he did that it would really justify the young man sitting before him killing him.

"Who—who are—are you talking about, man? I'm lost here— gimme something to go on. Maybe—maybe I can make things right."

Fear's eyebrows slanted and his nose scrunched up. The corner of his top lip twitched hostilely. "Her name is Constance—and there's not a goddamn thang you can do to make it right."

"*Constance?* Constance. That's my baby girl! I haven't seen her in years—what could I have done to—" Radcliff's words suddenly died in his mouth when he realized how he'd wronged his daughter.

It finally became clear why Fear was there now. He'd come to claim his life for him giving Constance away to a pimp to pay for his drug debt. Radcliff remembered how he'd been beating himself up for what he'd done to his baby girl. The havoc his conscience wreaked on him drove him to stay high around the clock. He hated being sober because it would leave him aware of what he did, and he wasn't trying to feel anything. Once he even tried to hang himself, but the beam in the basement ceiling gave and he hit the floor.

"Uh-huh, shit is finally clicking upstairs for you, ain't it?"

Radcliff broke down sobbing aloud, tears flooding his cheeks by the buckets. His eyes had turned pink and snot oozed out of his right nose, coming dangerously close to his top lip. "Oh, my God! You've gotta tell her I'm so sorry! Tell her I've never forgiven myself for what happened! I'm—I'm her father and I shoulda protected her, but instead—," he snorted up the snot. "But instead, I chose to give her away 'cause of my own selfish neeedddsss—" He broke down sobbing harder, placing his hand over the lower half of his face. His shoulder rocked as he cried and cried.

Fear looked to his left rolling his eyes and taking a breath. He appeared to be annoyed by Radcliff's emotional tantrum. "Nigga, spare me the theatrics. You weren't that broken up when you gave her to that ol' pimping-ass nigga, now were you?" Fear mad dogged him as he waited for his response.

Radcliff stopped sobbing, but he didn't respond. He actually did feel remorse for what he'd done, but not as much as he was leading the assassin to believe.

"I thought so." He unsheathed a hunting knife from somewhere on his waistline and stabbed it into the tabletop, leaving it standing upright. Then, he laid his Glock down beside it. "Like it or not, you're gonna die tonight. It's as simple as that. But luckily for you, I'm nice enough to give you the option of how you'll meet your end. You've gotta knife or gun to choose from. Now, if I were you, I'd choose the gun. A bullet will make your death quick and clean. Trust me, I know how to make it where you won't feel a thing. Everything will just suddenly go black, and that will be the end of it. So, what will it be, Mr. Smith?"

Radcliff shut his eyes briefly, as he swallowed the lump of

fear in his throat. He weighed his options when it came to ending his life. He couldn't imagine a knife being less painful than a bullet, so he opted to go along with being shot. Reluctantly, he nodded to the gun.

"Excellent choice." Fear stood upright, sheathing his knife, and walking toward Radcliff. "Get on your knees and make peace with the Big Man in the sky," he commanded Radcliff.

The crackhead got down on his knees and interlocked his fingers, staring up at the ceiling. Fear pointed his gun at the back of his skull while listening to his prayer.

"Father God, I kneel before You knowing I have sinned against You in so many different ways. In what I have said and done, as well as in the dirty thoughts that flood through my mind. I know that I am a sinner and as such, I was the cause of the Lord Jesus being crucified on the cruel cross to—" Radcliff cried profusely and trembled as he recited the prayer. He was petrified of dying and didn't know what to expect before he met his end. Seeing the gun in his face became too much for him so he shut his eyes, continuing to recite the prayer. *"Take the punishment that I justly deserve, to pay that price for my sins. Lord, I know I am unworthy to come before You, but I ask Your forgiveness of all my sins, for the sake of Your Son, Jesus Christ Who died for me at Calvary."*

Fear was about to pull the trigger until something on the countertop caught his eye. It looked to be some kind of letter of some sort. He picked up the letter and read it over. The document was informing a Radcliff Smith that he was in stage four of pancreas cancer, and it had unfortunately spread. Fear sat the letter back on the countertop. He stared down at Radcliff's pitiful face debating whether he should go ahead and pop him or not.

Radcliff continued with his prayer. After a while, he became curious as to why the stranger hadn't knocked his head off and opened his eyes, one by one. His forehead creased confusingly when he noticed Fear wasn't standing over him. It was as if he'd vanished. Slowly, Radcliff got up on his feet and looked around the kitchen for him, but he didn't find him. He then looked up at the ceiling, crossing himself in the sign of the holy crucifix and thanking God for sparing his life.

***

Fear made his way out of Radcliff's house and slid in behind the wheel of his car, slamming the door shut. Constance was staring at him like she was waiting for him to say something. He looked at her and he could tell that the anticipation was killing her. He wondered how she'd feel if he told her that he'd put her father out of his misery. There was one thing to want thing to wish someone was dead, it was another thing having them actually be killed. For all, he knew her feelings may have changed in regards of her old man. So, he wasn't sure how he should tell her about the decision he'd ultimately made.

"Well—did you do it?" Constance asked him, waiting anxiously to hear his reply.

Fear stared into her eyes for what seemed like an eternity, weighing his options. Finally, having decided on what he was going to tell her, he nodded. Instantly, her eyes filled with tears, and they came streaming down her cheeks. She snatched him into an affectionate hug, shutting her eyes. A grin spread across her lips.

A confused look spread across Fear's face. He wasn't sure how she'd taken the news. "Are you—are you sad?"

Constance broke her embrace and started wiping her dripping eyes. "No. I'm far from sad. These are—these are tears of joy. I can't believe you did this for me. You actually gave all of those people the business 'cause they used, abused, and left me emotionally scarred. That's proof—," her voice became overwhelmed with emotion and started to crack.

Seeing more tears coming down her cheeks, Fear took a few napkins out of the armrest and handed them to her. She wiped her wet face with them. "That's proof that you do care about me."

"Of course, I do. You my people, slim," Fear assured her, seriousness dripping from his eyes and vocal cords. "If anyone fucks wit' chu, they're fucking with me. Straight like that. We're family."

A smile came across her face and she looked at him, excitedly. "You mean like husband and wife?"

"Deeper than that, slim, I'm talking 'bout some next level shit. Our shit runs deeper than blood and bonds. You Griff me, lil' mama?"

Constance stared at him with googly eyes, looking like a lovesick puppy. "I love you—" she said, waiting for his response.

Fear was taken aback by what she had said. He didn't know what to make of it. He didn't know if she meant like the love you had for a homie or brother, or the other kind of love. You know, that love a woman has for her man or her husband. He figured she couldn't possibly mean that she loved him romantically. They hadn't known each other that long for her to catch feelings like that. On top of that, she knew he had a fiancé and how much deeply he felt about her.

"I love you, too," Fear finally said.

Constance smiled harder, suddenly kissing him on the mouth. She tried to make out with him, but he held her at arm's length. Her reaction to him saying, *"I love you!"* back let him know how he'd fucked up saying it back. He was sure she was confused about what kind of love he meant, but he didn't have the heart to break it to her, right now. He figured the next time the L word came up; he'd tell her his true feelings toward her.

"Relax, lil' mama, we've gotta get outta here. You know what I just laid down in there," he referred to him lying about killing Radcliff inside of the house.

"Oh, right," Constance said, as she laid her head against the passenger window, smiling. It felt good being in love with someone that loved her back. It was a feeling she never wanted to lose, and she'd kill anyone that tried to take it away from her.

***

Fear had gotten another call on his business cell phone for

another lick. His assignment was to knock off the leader of this Jamaican drug clique called Da Rude Bwois. Da Rude Bwois was run by this cutthroat Rasta named Don Dada. The Rastafarians were making a lot of money in their section over in the Ladera Heights area, dealing coke, dope, and weed. The problem was while Da Rude Bwois were doing their thing over there, they were stepping on the competition's toes. You know, fucking up their bag!

Anyway, Fear got a call to step in and handle things. Ladera Heights is known as the Black Beverly Hills to those that reside in Los Angeles County. The entire area was occupied by white families at one time, but all that changed over the years. The Heights had a below-average violent crime rate and just above average property crime rate. The nigga that hired Fear for the hit wanted to keep it that way, so he paid him a little extra to make sure he disposed of Don Dada's body. Knowing how niggaz couldn't resist a bad bitch.

Fear used Constance to get close to the leader of the Da Rude Bwois. She played the damsel-in-distress, claiming that her car had broken down and she needed to use his cell phone to call Triple-A. Don Dada happily unlocked his door to let her inside, and as soon as he did, Fear barged in and slit his throat. From there he went on to show Constance how to drain a body of its blood, chop it up, bag it and dispose of it. While she was busy taking care of Don Dada's corpse, Fear busied himself with going through the Rasta's apartment. He found four bricks of coke and two bricks of Mexican black tar heroin.

Plus, a number of guns, all of which he stashed inside a pillowcase and took with him. He and Constance had bagged Don Dada's severed body parts inside black garbage bags. He then dropped them off to an acquaintance of Master Hahn who worked at a mortuary, so he could burn them to ashes. Afterward, they took the spoils of the lick home. Constance whipped Fear up a fantastic dinner and dipped to Wal-Mart to pick herself up some feminine hygiene products.

Fear laid back on the couch as *Good Times* played on the flat-screen TV. His hand had a loose hold on a Heineken. His eyes were narrowed and every couple of minutes his head would drop as he dozed off. For the umpteenth time, he'd nearly spilled his beer onto his lap and every time he almost did, he'd wake up just in time to catch it.

No more than twenty minutes prior, he had devoured a hearty meal of T-bone steak, shrimp, cheese potatoes, and a Caesar salad. No sooner than he drank half his beer, The Itis had taken him. He'd had hopes of catching up on his favorite show growing up, but the Sandman had paid him a visit.

Hearing his cell phone ring woke Fear from his sleep. He swallowed the last of his Heineken and sat the bottle down on the coffee table. He picked the cell phone up and saw the call was *Blocked*. He started not to answer it, but something told him he should. Fear pressed *answer* and placed the cell phone to his ear.

"What's up with it?" he spoke. The caller said something, but he couldn't hear him over the blare of the show's theme music. "Hold on, family. Let me turn this TV off. I can't hear you," Fear told the caller. He turned it off. "Now, what were you saying?"

"I said, *you're* a dead man, mayate!" The caller hung up.

Fear saw a masked gunman standing behind him through the tinted black glass of the television, raising a ratchet to the back of his head. Using lightning-fast reflexes, he snatched the bottle and broke the end of it off at the edge of the coffee table. Just as the masked man pointed the gun, Fear sliced him across the wrist.

"Arghhhhh!" he gritted his teeth. Feeling a burning sensation in his wrist, he dropped his weapon.

"You break into my house, mothafucka!" Fear barked with arched eyebrows and a crinkled nose. His lips were twisted, and veins were bulging in his neck.

He snatched the man over the couch and turned him around. He pulled his chin back and exposed his throat. He stabbed the broken half of the green glass bottle into his neck with a grunt, and dragged it around to the other end, spilling a crimson fountain.

"Argggg!" the intruder gurgled as his mouth filled with blood and quickly overflowed it, splattering on the cushions of the beige couch.

Chapter Twelve

Bathoom! Bathoom!

The door rattled and Fear's head snapped up, seeing the door lurch back and forth. The only thing keeping it from swinging inward was the chain, but then—*Boom!* Two more masked men spilled in, ratchets in hand.

Fear snatched the dead man's blood speckled blower from off the couch and hoisted him up to use as a human shield.

Choot! Choot! Choot! Choot! Choot! Choot!

Bullets whizzed through the air, narrowly missing him, pelting the dead body of the masked man that Fear used as a human shield and tattering the back of the couch. The masked men let off in unison, trying to air their target the fuck out. Fear hunched behind the slab of mutilated flesh, keeping his head down and waiting for a chance to respond as the bullets flew all around him. Seeing his chance to react, he responded with bursts of rapid gunfire.

Choot! Choot! Choot!

Waves of heat snatched off the left side of one of the masked gunners' faces, tore off his bottom jaw, and left a gaping hole through the center of his forehead. He dropped to the floor dead, his soul spiraling toward that inferno below ground. Fear swept his blower around to the last shooter and let loose.

Choot! Choot! Choot!

"Ahhhhhhhh!"

When the first bullet hit him in the neck, he grimaced like he was about to bite something and slapped a hand over the spurting hole. The second one struck his chest and the last marred his shoulder. Fear closed one eye and took aim before sending that third one at him. There was a whistle and then splat, the shooter's blood and chunks of his brain went flying out the back of his skull. When that shit hit the hardwood floor, it looked like someone's vomit. The lifeless man hit the surface right after the killa's human shield did once Fear released him.

Fear advanced upon the two masked men he'd dispatched cautiously. He kneeled to them and pulled off their ski-masks, tossing them aside. Lines creased his forehead as he realized he recognized them. They were Gustavo's men.

Choot!

Fear grimaced as he took one in the back. He whipped around and there was a fourth masked assailant that had entered his apartment. Fear noticed the opened window at the end of the hallway, ruffling the sheer curtains with a cool breeze passing through. Fear realized he'd gotten inside of the apartment through the fire escape.

Fear went to lift his gun, but the assailant had the drop on him. He sent a hot-one through Fear's thigh, causing him to drop his gun when he went to clutch his leg. The assailant took his sweet time approaching, taking shot after shot at him.

Choot! Choot!

Two shots slammed Fear up against the wall, but one more left him bleeding on the floor on his side. Seeing the gunman moving in to finish him, he reached for the gun he'd dropped. His palm had just grazed its handle when the intruder mashed his boot against his hand, pinning it to the handle. He looked up at the gunman who had just pointed his silenced .380 between his eyes. A wicked smile formed on his lips.

He pulled off his mask and his malicious eyes penetrated Fear's. "Adios, primo," he said.

The gunman's malicious expression melted into one of confusion and excruciation. His eyes bulged and when his lips peeled apart, a red river spilled over them. Dropping his silenced .380 to the floor, he slowly turned around as he grabbed at his back.

Looking up, Fear saw a butcher's knife buried down to its handle in the man's back. When he peered beyond him, he saw Constance lunge forth, gripping a meat cleaver with both hands. She released a snarl right before she buried the cleaver in his face, nearly splitting it in half. Blood poured out of the split in his face and splashed on his black thermal. He dropped to his knees and fell on the side of his face, dead.

"Oh, my God, baby! What did they do to you?" Constance said, seeing Fear lying on the floor bleeding like a stuck pig.

She grabbed the cordless telephone and dialed 911. She then tossed the telephone aside and rushed to his aide. She laid his head into her lap and caressed his head.

He tried to talk, but she hushed him. "Shhhh, don't say anything, save your strength." She placed a tender kiss on his forehead and continued to stroke his head. "Everything is going to be all right, baby. You just hang in there."

"Hide the guns—hide the—hide the drugs." Fear's eyes blinked and he coughed up blood, struggling to escape the cold hands of Death. His crimson hand grasped Constance's hand, squeezing tightly. "Stash—stash—stash the money." He stared up into her eyes in what could very well be his last hour.

"Alright, alright." Constance nodded, wiping her tears with a curled finger. She ran back and forth across the apartment gathering what he'd told her to and stashing it in the secret compartments inside the unit.

***

The jail had been on lockdown for several weeks since the riot had broken out. Gunplay, Two-Bit, Lethal, and all their crews were sent to segregation. Well, those of their crews that weren't seriously wounded and needed medical attention. Even with all that had gone down, there was still a bounty on Lethal's head. A bounty that Lethal and Two-Bit aimed to collect by any means necessary.

Gunplay was shadowboxing when he heard the slot in his cell's door slide open. When he turned around, he locked eyes with a pair of very familiar eyes. They belonged to his homeboy from his set. He worked as a corrections officer for the jail.

"It's time, young nigga, strap up!" The corrections officer told him before unlocking the door.

Gunplay got hurriedly dressed and grabbed his Bone Crusher, a big ass jail-made knife responsible for many fatalities. When Gunplay's cell door open, he strolled out and dapped up with his older homeboy. The corrections officer shut his cell door and walked him towards the cell Lethal was holed up in.

"This fool up in there?" Gunplay inquired.

"Nah, I crushed two ten mg of Ambien in his food, knocked his monkey-ass out cold," the corrections officer told him. "Your job will be easy from here on out, cuz. All you gotta do is slit the mothafucka's throat, and call yo' folks so we can get paid."

Although Gunplay had set it up for his homies to be in on Lethal's demise, things didn't end up working out that way. He hadn't expected for Lethal to jump-start a riot that would put the jail on lockdown. That play he'd laid down had thrown a wrench in his plan, so now he had to alternate his original plan. Now, he was going to be the only one to catch a body, and the loot that Fear hit him with was going to be divided between his homeboys. Sure, he'd see a smaller cut from it, but he was still going to eat regardless. Besides, he didn't want to be the only one eating out of his clique. He believed in the mantra, *Feed the wolves or the wolves will eat you.*

"Cuz, I wanna handle this nigga, but to cut the nigga's throat while he's sleeping? That's some real lowlife shit, my nigga. There ain't no honor in that, you feel me?" Gunplay told the corrections officer.

He'd always killed honorably. The fools he'd gotten at knew he was coming for them. He never snuck a nigga in his life. They all seen him coming, and that's the way he liked it.

The corrections officer took a deep breath and he unlocked Lethal's cell door. He then turned to Gunplay and placed a reassuring hand on his shoulder, saying, "Look, loc, I know where you coming from and I respect it. But you said yo folks said that this lil' mothafucka is a trained killa. He's not no joke, so I can see you getting down on this hit like you're about to. Now, if he was a regular old street nigga like you and I, then I'd say wait 'til this nigga is up and alert to do 'em. In this situation, unfortunately, that's not the case."

Gunplay lowered his head and massaged his chin thinking on the situation at hand. Everything that his OG homie was saying was right. Lethal wasn't some regular old street nigga he was dealing with. Homeboy was a professional hitman. He killed on a different level than any of his enemies or the circle he ran in. So, it was best that he handled him in the way that was presented to him.

"Alright, cuz, fuck it!" Gunplay said. "Let's get this shit over with."

"That's what I'm talking about. Work smarter not harder." The corrections officer nudged him affectionately and opened the Lethal's cell door.

They found him lying on his stomach asleep with his wrists handcuffed at his back. All Gunplay had to do was put him out of his misery and call Fear so he could collect that dough he'd promised him. The hit would be a piece of cake. As a matter of fact, it would be far easier than Gunplay's plan of killing him.

"There he is, cuz, nigga sleeping like a newborn baby." He glanced at his timepiece and then looked at Gunplay. "Gon' get that shit over with, gangsta. I gotta go back to making my rounds in the next couple of minutes."

Gunplay was about to walk into Lethal's cell and finish him off. He stopped short once he heard a familiar voice down the corridor.

"I thought I told you before that homeboy's life is mine."

Gunplay and the corrections officers looked down the hallway. Another corrections officer was removing the shackles from around Two-Bit's wrists. The white kid was staring at Gunplay wearing a devilish smile on his face, looking like a straight-up psycho serial killa.

"I don't give a rat's ass what chu told me before, homeboy. I laid claim to cuz life, and it's gonna be me that takes it. Anyone that gets in my way is asking for an early grave, feel me?"

Gunplay kept his eyes on Two-Bit, as he spat on the floor.

The corrections officer finished removing the handcuffs from Two-Bit's wrists. The corrections officer with Two-Bit held an affiliation to the Bloods just like him. He was what the other corrections officer was to Gunplay. They both were getting paid from this situation.

"If you don't back away from that cell, I'm gonna put chu in the same grave you're talking about putting me in," Two-Bit assured him, as he massaged his aching wrists. The corrections officer had put the handcuffs on too tight.

"Is that a fact?" Gunplay stepped out into the center of the hallway shank held at his side.

"Big fact!" Two-Bit told him. He kept his eyes on Gunplay, as the corrections officer passed him a shank of his own.

"I challenge you to a game of death," Gunplay scowled, as he addressed Two-Bit. "The winner takes homeboy's life and whatever money that's on his head."

Two-Bit cleaned the dirt from underneath his fingernails with his shank. He was still smiling devilishly, as he performed the task. He seldom broke eye contact with Gunplay. "You're in luck, homeboy, I'm always up for a challenge." His face balled up angrily, ready to engage in combat.

"Ooooh, this is about to get bloody," the corrections officer that had escorted Two-Bit said.

He smiled and rubbed his hands together. He was sure the knife fight was going to be better than anything he'd seen on pay-per-view.

"This is definitely going to get interesting," the corrections officer with Gunplay stated.

The corrections officer on Two-Bit's side whistled for the other corrections officer's attention. He looked up to see him holding up a few blue-faced one-hundred-dollar bills. "I got three hunnit that says my white boy gets the best of yo' black boy."

The corrections officer on Gunplay's side chuckled and pulled out a folded wad of money. He unfolded it and counted out fifteen twenty-dollar bills, holding it up for his co-worker to see. "Shiiittt, negro, you ain't said nothing but a word. Bet."

"Aaaaaah!" Two-Bit charged down the hallway at Gunplay.

"Aaaaaah!" Gunplay charged down the hallway at Two-Bit.

***

As Italia laid in bed, in a coma, the machines that were attached to her body made eerie noises as some kept her alive, while others kept a monitor on her vitals. Her breasts rose and fell easily as she breathed. The fingers of the hand that was hooked to her I.V. began to twitch. First, it was the pinky finger, and then the finger next to it. The fingers of the wrist that her identification bracelet was on began to twitch as well. Afterward, her eyelids started twitching and her heart monitor showed more activity.

***

Fear survived his wounds and recovered at UCLA hospital. As soon as he was released, it was back to business as usual for him and Constance. They stayed putting in work, stacking dead bodies and bankrolls along the way. Although they were waist-deep in the streets, they kept a low profile. They still had Gustavo to deal with, and they wouldn't be able to relax until he was a corpse. Constance recalled Lester telling them about the two-hundred-and-fifty-thousand-dollar bounty on Fear's head. She knew once Fear was dead, she wouldn't have to spend the rest of her life looking over her shoulders. On top of that, she'd be two-hundred-and-fifty-thousand dollars richer. That was a lot of scratch for a bitch like her. She'd never had that much dough in her life.

After convincing herself what needed to be done, Constance retrieved her black .45 semi-automatic handgun and screwed the silencer on its barrel. She made sure it was locked and loaded before making her way around the house looking for Fear. She located him in the garage lifting dumbbells. His muscular back was turned to her and he was covered in beads of sweat. His muscular, vein riddled arms bulged with each curl of the dumbbells he made.

Constance was so stealthy with her approach he didn't hear her coming up behind him. That's until Fear looked at the ground and saw her shadow. Huffing and puffing out of breath, he dropped the dumbbells and turned around. He was shocked when Constance lifted her .45 semi-automatic handgun.

***

Pedro was shooting a game of pool with one of the goons. Spectators watched from the sidelines taking swigs of beer and chatting amongst one another.

Pedro put the last of his striped balls into one of the netted, black leather pockets and circled the pool table. His eyes were focused on what pocket to put the 8-ball in and what angle he was going to take the shot from. Figuring what side he was going to take the shot from, he called it out and leaned over the pool table. His eyes zeroed in on the shiny black ball and he teased his stick, hitting it. The tip of the stick jabbed the 8-ball. The 8-ball made a—*crack* sound as it nicked the side of a red ball, en route to the pocket Pedro called out.

The 8-ball dropped inside of the pocket and Pedro smiled, victoriously. He stood upright and snatched the thousand dollars he had riding on the bet. He looked to his opponent who wore a look of defeat. He decided to rub his win in his face by kissing the stack of blue faces and shoving them in his pocket.

"Better luck next time, poppy." Pedro smiled.

Right then, another one of the goons walked inside the pool hall through the backdoor. He approached Pedro and whispered something into his ear that made his face turn serious.

"Okay, then, let her in," Pedro told him. He sharpened the tip of his pool stick as he watched the goon walk away. "Yo', Titon lock that front door, man! Gordo, kill that jukebox, homie," he gave orders to his underlings, and they went off to do like they were told.

"What's up?" a goon asked while holding a beer and leaning against the bar.

"We've finally got our hands on that mayate that's been a pain in our asses," Pedro announced for everyone gathered to hear. Every man present was a part of Gustavo's organization so there wasn't a big secret they were gunning for Fear.

"'Bout fucking time," the goon said and placed his bottle of beer on the bar top. He then started over in Pedro's direction.

The sounds of grunting and sporadic footsteps drew the gathering of Pedro and the others. They stood as a collective watching one of their own and someone else bringing in someone covered by a blanket. The pair emerged into the pool hall carrying the dead weight. They were grimacing and their foreheads were coated in sweat.

"Lay him over here!" Pedro told them, tapping his stick against the pool table he'd just won the game on.

The pair carried the body over to the table and dumped it. They then hunched over with their hands on their knees panting out of breath. Pedro laid his stick beside the body as he walked around the pool table. For the first time, he got a good look at the person that brought in the cadaver. To his surprise, it was an African American woman with locs spilling out of the opening of her hood. He had expected the person looking to collect the bounty to be a man. But clearly, she had a set of balls on her.

Still panting, the woman wiped her sweaty forehead and threw her head back at him like, *What's up?* He returned the gesture as he stepped around the body. One of the goons produced a gun from underneath his shirt and stood guard at the hallway that led to the backdoor. The rest of them held their guns down at their sides. If they smelled something fishy, they were going to pump homegirl full of some hot shit.

Pedro withdrew the blanket from the upper half of the corpse and revealed Fear's lifeless face. Although the dead man looked like the killa, he had to be sure before he reported back to Gustavo. He pulled out his cell phone and brought up the picture his boss sent him of the assassin. He held the cell phone right beside the face of the cadaver and compared them. A wicked smile spread across his face seeing that they were identical.

"Is it him?" one of the goons asked.

"Yeah, is that the Vato we've been looking for?" another goon asked.

Pedro nodded as he dialed Gustavo, excited to tell him the good news. "Yeah, it's him," he confirmed to the others. "I gotta admit. I expected him to be shorter, though. He's actually bigger than what he appears in the picture jefe sent." Pedro brought his cellular to his ear.

When Gustavo answered, he told him the good news in Spanish and could hear the joy in his voice. He promptly asked for a picture for confirmation and he shot him one. He told Pedro that the picture he gave him was definitely Fear. Pedro disconnected the call and put his cell phone away. He looked to the African American woman and told her happily that it was the man they'd been looking for. She smiled and rubbed her hands together greedily, knowing she was about to get mad gwap for her troubles.

Abruptly, Pedro pulled out his gun and pointed it at her. His eyebrows were slanted, and his nose was scrunched up. The woman's eyes widen fearfully, and her hands shot up in the air. She swallowed a lump in her throat and regretted trying to collect her due.

"Sorry, Mija, but there's no dinero—" Pedro continued to mean mug her, but then suddenly, he busted up laughing. "I'm playing wit' chu, mommy, relax." He smiled and tucked his gun. She lowered her hands and took a breath, sighing with relief. "Titon, fetch me that fettia!" Pedro referred to the bounty money.

Titon disappeared behind the bar and returned with a duffle bag. He tossed it over to Pedro, who in turn, tossed it over to the woman.

The woman glanced inside the duffle bag and smiled at her small fortune. She zipped the duffle bag back up, grasped its handles, and bid Pedro a farewell. As she was making her departure, Pedro called her back and she looked over her shoulder.

"What's your name, mommy?" Pedro asked curiously.

"Constance," she answered and proceeded toward the hallway.

Pedro gave the goon blocking the hallway entrance a nod and

he moved out of her way. Constance disappeared down the hallway with the goon following behind her to lock the backdoor.

Constance turned out to be a Judas and proof you couldn't trust anyone!

Tranay Adams

Chapter Thirteen

Gustavo sat in the back of his Mercedes-Benz limousine. He took pulls of his Cuban cigar and blew out clouds of smoke. A smile was plastered across his face. He was feeling victorious since he was able to squash Fear like a cockroach. He only had two regrets. One, he wasn't the one that put the bullet in him that ended his life. Two, he felt awful for allowing his nephew, Ezra to talk him into allowing him to go after Fear. He hadn't heard from him since he went after the assassin that night, and he was pretty sure he was dead.

Wherever you lay, Sobrino, I hope you're in peace, Gustavo thought. Although there were quite a few casualties on his end due to the ongoing conflict with Fear, he wasn't going to spend his time complaining.

He'd learned a long time ago that you had to take your wins where you could get them. All that mattered now was he was free to focus on expanding his empire and making more money than he had before.

A knock on the back tinted window drew Gustavo's attention. He let the window down and came face to face with Pedro.

"The perimeter is clear, jefe. You can come in now," Pedro reported to Gustavo. Gustavo nodded and put the window back up. He mashed out his cigar, grabbed his crutches, and got out of the limousine. Pedro escorted him inside the barbershop.

As soon as they entered the small bell hanging over the door rang. There was a thirty-inch television mounted on the wall that was playing a basketball game. The shop was empty except for the Dominican kid who was busy washing his hands at the sink. He was a short, brown-skinned cat with cornrows and a goatee. He was dressed in a powder blue shirt. The name tag on the opposite side of his breast pocket read, Angel.

Gustavo frowned as he looked around the barbershop. He couldn't help wondering why he didn't see Old Man Reyes there. He was the owner of the joint. The seventy-four-year-old man had been cutting his hair since he was five. Since he had become a teenager, he saw him every Friday for his regular haircut and shave. He had been there every day to groom him rain, sleet, or snow. Even when Gustavo couldn't make it down to the shop, he'd make home visits to take care of him.

"Hey!" Gustavo called out to the young man. Angel dried his hands and turned around to him, wearing a smile. He seemed to be a really jovially person based on the expression written across his face. The kid raised his eyebrows as if to ask, *What's up?* "Where the hell is the old man?"

"Oh, you must mean, unc," Angel said. "Well, he and his wife left the country to celebrate their fiftieth anniversary. So, he left me here to run the shop. He showed me exactly how you like your hair cut and wanted me to assure you that you're in good hands."

Gustavo gave Angel the side-eye. He wasn't too sure how he felt about letting him cut his hair and all. The old man had spoiled him, and he'd gotten used to him taking care of his grooming needs. On the other hand, Mr. Reyes was getting up in age and time wasn't exactly on his side. He was sure in the next couple of years he'd be looking for someone else to cut his hair. So, he may as well try the kid out and see how he liked him.

"Where are my manners? You'll have to excuse me. I'm Mr. Reyes' nephew, Angel." Angel extended his hand and Gustavo reluctantly shook it. "You're Gustavo, right?"

"Right." Gustavo propped his crutches against a neighboring barber's chair. Using his good leg, he hobbled over to Angel's chair and sat down.

Once he laid back in the chair, Angel flapped out a smock and draped it around his neck. He buttoned the smock at the back of his neck and went on to prepare him for the shave. Angel wrapped Gustavo's face with a warm, wet towel to lay down his facial hair.

"Pedro, why don't you relax and take a load off? Don't be so uptight. We're amongst a friend." That being said, Pedro sat down to watch the basketball game.

***

Five minutes later

Gustavo lay back in the barber's chair with a face foamed with shaving cream, snoring. He slowly began to stir awake, hearing the straight razor being sharpened against a strap. His eyes fluttered open and he sat up, snorting, wiping the drool from the corner of his lips. When his vision came into focus, he almost shit himself seeing Angel standing before him holding the sharp blade. His face was balled up and he was smiling devilishly. He looked totally different from the upbeat young man he encountered when he first entered the barbershop. Suddenly, Angel reached under his chin and pulled back his skin, bringing along his face and cornrows. He had been wearing a mask all along. The entire time it had been Fear wearing a disguise. Gustavo went to scream, but before the sound could leave his lips the razor swiped across his thick, flat nose.

Snikt!

His severed nose went flying across the shop and sliding across the floor, leaving a smear of blood. Fear spun the barber's chair around, leaving the Mexican kingpin face to face with his horrifying reflection. His eyes bulged and his mouth widened. He couldn't believe that it was him he was staring back at. He looked like a Mr. Potato Head without the attachable nose.

"Ahhhhhhh!" He bellowed as he stared at the mutilated image in the mirror. His wails of terror were quickly cut short when the straight razor slipped under his chin and yanked around. The soft flesh of his throat split and a black river of blood flowed. "Gaggggaaaa!" He stuck out his tongue and went cockeyed as he grabbed for his neck. His blood-drenched his white dress shirt and stained his light gray suit.

"That'll be twelve dollars," Fear said, staring at his handiwork through the mirror.

He watched the chunky Mexican bleed out until he went still.

Afterward, he washed off the razor and his hands. He gave himself the once over in the mirror, checking his nostrils for long hairs and his teeth for food. Once he was done, he closed the razor, stuck it into his back pocket, and headed for the door. On his way out of the door, he passed Pedro who was slumped in a chair, with his back to the window of the shop. His eyes were wide and vacant while his mouth hung open. His throat had been slit from ear to ear. Blood had run from the slash in his neck and stained the collar of his white button-down pink.

When she'd recalled the bounty, Gustavo had on Fear's head, Constance came up with a plan for her to collect. She remembered when the assassin had told her about his sociopath cousin, Malik that had gotten plastic surgery to look identical to him. She got the location where he was buried from him and dug his body up. Luckily for her, Malik's corpse wasn't badly decomposed. He still looked like he'd only been dead for a few hours. The only difference between him and Fear was their height. She just hoped that Gustavo wouldn't notice that. Fortunately, the Mexican kingpin didn't suspect anything suspicious. He totally bought her story about murking Fear for a bag, and he was happy to give her the two-hundred and fifty grand for her troubles.

Without having to worry about Gustavo being on his ass, Fear was left to hash a plan to take him out of the game permanently. He did his homework and was able to find out where Gustavo got his haircut. He also found out that the old man that cut his hair, Mr. Reyes was falling behind on paying his taxes on his barbershop. Fear paid the old head a visit. He offered him the dough to keep the shop open in exchange of him setting up Gustavo. Old Man Reyes agreed, and the rest was history.

Fear took one last look over his shoulder before pushing through the door, causing the bell above to ring as he made his exit. Pulling his cellular from his breast pocket, he made a transaction that made a ten-thousand-dollar deposit into Old Man Reyes bank account. He opened the trunk of Gustavo's Mercedes-Benz limousine and grabbed a duffle bag out of it. Next, he hopped into the backseat of the luxury vehicle and slammed the door shut. The partition that separated him from the chauffeur rolled down and Constance looked over her shoulder at him. She removed the black chauffeur's cap she was wearing, pulled off the band that held her hair together, and shook her locs loose. She combed her fingers through her locs and smiled at him.

"Where are we headed now?" Constance asked him. Gustavo was so mesmerized by the presumed death of Fear he hadn't noticed his usual driver wasn't behind the wheel. Constance had knocked him out cold and left him slumped inside of an alley.

"UCLA Hospital," Fear told her. He leaned over and un-zipped his duffle bag, pulling out a fresh set of clothes. He was on his way to see Italia and he wanted to be looking his best.

Constance rolled her eyes and rolled the partition back up. She was really jealous of the way he felt about Italia. She wished that he felt the same way about her, but he obviously didn't. She hated that shit. She wanted him all to herself, and she'd stop at nothing to make him hers, even if it meant killing Italia's pretty ass.

Fear had gotten fully dressed in his fresh set of clothes by the time Constance pulled away from the curb. He sprayed Cool Water cologne on his neck and wrists, rubbing them together. He dumped his old set of clothing inside the duffle bag along with the cologne. He then zipped the bag up and set it aside. Right then, his cellular started ringing. He looked at the screen and saw he was getting a video-call from Gunplay. As soon as Fear accepted the call, he found himself looking at Lethal. He was inside the shower room. He was surrounded by hardened convicts. They all wore T-shirts over their heads with their eyes peering out through the neck holes of them. There were eight men in total. All of whom were armed with either twelve-inch steel pipes or knives they'd fashioned on the floor of their cells.

Lethal pulled off his shirt and threw it aside. He was now in his undershirt. He hiked up his pants as he spread his legs, getting into a martial-arts fighting stance. The first convict ran at him and swung his pipe at his head. Lethal ducked and punched him so hard he flew backward, dropping his pipe. Another convict ran up from behind him. Lethal swung around and kicked him hard across the jaw. The convict's body spun around in a one-hundred-and-eighty degree turn and he dropped to the floor, releasing his knife.

Lethal swung back around and punched another convict in the face. As soon as his fist connected, a fourth convict cracked him across the back of the head. Lethal winced as he stumbled forward. A fifth convict cracked him across the jaw with his pipe. The swift blow sent a couple of his broken teeth flying and his blood splattering against the wall. Lethal's eyes rolled to their whites. Before he could hit the floor, a sixth convict ran forward and swung his pipe with all his might. When the pipe connected Lethal's scalp split open to the white meat and his blood dotted the floor.

A seventh and eighth convict rushed him up against the wall with knives. Holding him there, they stabbed him viciously and without remorse. Lethal hit the shower floor, but he was still breathing. The ten convicts rushed him. They beat him with their pipes and stabbed him with their knives until they were panting out of breath. When they were finished with Lethal there were bloodstains all over their shirts, and their weapons were dripping blood.

"Hold this for me, cuz," Gunplay, who was filming everything, passed his contraband cell phone to one of the ten convicts.

The convict, in turn, passed him his knife. Fear watched as Gunplay, who was also wearing a T-shirt over his head, pulled Lethal up from the floor by his hair. Gustavo's enforcer was a bloody fucking mess. The side of his head was indented while the other side bore two knots, one bigger than the other. His left eye was swollen shut, his nose was twisted to the side, every tooth in his mouth was broken, and he had several stab wounds in his face. The blood that drenched his face had spilled down onto his undershirt's collar and stained it pink. Lethal's good eye stared out at nothing and his mouth moved animatedly. It was a miracle that he was still alive and breathing. He was one tough son of a bitch! No one would argue that.

"Look into the camera!" Gunplay ordered as he pointed his

knife at the convict holding his cell phone. "Look at it, motha-fucka!" Lethal moaned and continued to bleed out. His good eye lazily moved over and looked into the camera lens of the cellular. "This is what happens when you fuck with the big homie," he informed Lethal before sawing into his throat with the knife and spilling blood everywhere.

The sharpened blade went through warm flesh, muscle, and tendon before it finally met bone. Clenching his jaws, Gunplay continued to saw at Lethal's neck until his body fell forward. Once he'd completed the deed, he was left holding the enforcer's severed head which he held up for Fear to see. Gunplay looked like one of those terrorists from Iraq wearing that T-shirt over his head. The crimson splatters on his shirt, accompanied by the blood dripping from his hands, only added to his nightmarish look.

"You see this, cuz?" Gunplay looked back and forth between the cell phone and Lethal's severed head. "This is love, right here! I love you, my nigga! And this gon' happen to any nigga that fucks wit' chu! That's my word! I put that on my dead locs!"

"Respect." Fear tapped his fist against his chest. He had mad love for Gunplay. He proved to be a stalwart young soldier, and he respected his gangsta to the fullest.

"Yo, cuz, throw that mothafucka over here!" one of the con-victs called out to Gunplay.

He gripped his pipe like it was a baseball bat and got into a swinger's stance. Gunplay threw Lethal's head like a baseball as best as he could. It zipped through the air. The convict swung his pipe with all his might. When the pipe impacted Lethal's head it sent blood and pieces of brain fragments flying everywhere. The head flew across the shower room and ricocheted off the wall, tumbling across the floor.

Afterward, another one of the convicts snatched the head up. They all threw the head around to each other and took turns hitting it with their pipes. Every last one of the convicts was serving life without parole for multiple homicides. They were all a bunch of incarcerated sociopaths, just like Gunplay. They lived for money and murder. Before they'd gotten locked up, they were in the streets putting in work for the set for free. Needless to say, they jumped at the opportunity to lay their murder game down for Gunplay for a fee.

Their families couldn't afford to send them money for commissary. So, they could use the five gees Gunplay was going to give them for the orchestrated hit.

Gunplay took the cell phone from the convict he'd given it to and walked away from the others. He listened closely to what Fear had to say to him.

"Yo, I'ma take care of you and yo guys first thing tomorrow morning," Fear assured him. He was going to drop the five-thousand dollars off to each of the relatives the convicts requested. He had to pay an additional ten grand to the corrections officers who set the entire thing up. The way he looked at it, it was money well spent since he'd finally gotten rid of Lethal.

"Fa sho'." Gunplay nodded as he paced the shower room, attention focused on the cell phone's screen.

"I don't want chu to worry about nothing, family. I hollered at my unc already so he's gonna make that happen," Fear assured.

"Good looking out, my nig."

"And I appreciate chu, young homie. I love you, nigga."

"I love you too, gangsta."

"Alright, fool, make sure you holla back at me." Fear disconnected the call.

"We're here," Constance announced. She'd just parked the limousine and stuck the visitor parking-card at the corner of the windshield.

Fear couldn't believe they'd made it out to UCLA Hospital so fast. He'd expected the ride to take longer than he did, but it obviously hadn't.

"Alright. I'll be right back," he told Constance, hopping out of the limousine and slamming the door shut behind him.

He walked inside the hospital and made it through the metal detectors without a hitch, likely because he'd left his gun inside the limousine. Fear walked into the gift shop. He scored a bouquet of the most beautiful red roses he'd ever seen, a *Get-Well* card, and a box of chocolates. He paid for the items and jumped on the elevator. Once he got off, he made it to Italia's room where he found her watching Love and Hip-hop. She'd awaken from her coma a few days ago and was well on her way to a full recovery.

As soon as she saw him, she smiled broadly. She was now fitted with a nasal cannula, which occupied both her nostrils to help her breathe. Italia wanted to say something to the love of her life, but her throat was still terribly sore from the breathing tube. She desperately wanted to hug, kiss, and rub all over her man and tell him how much she loved him. She was aching for him and couldn't wait to feel his warm embrace.

"Hey, baby, how're you doing?" Fear greeted Italia with a kiss on the forehead.

He showed her the things he'd purchased for her. He set the box of chocolates on her push-table, and then he read the card to her. The words the card presented were so sweet and sentimental it brought passionate tears to her eyes.

I want to go to the top of the mountains and just scream. I'm in love, so in love, met the girl of my dreams. I won't lie. I won't front. You're who I want, who I need. Without you, there's no me, you're The Air That I Breathe.

I love you, baby. Thank you for loving me when I could not love myself.

Alvin

She sniffled and tried to tell him she loved him. Unfortunately, due to her current state, she couldn't manage. Fear knew what she was trying to say, so he told her he loved her, too. Afterward, he took the old dead roses out of the see-through vase, which was sitting on the counter below the large window of the room. He tossed the dead flowers inside the trash can, dumped the water out of the vase, and refilled it with water from the faucet. He set the vase of water back on the counter and placed the fresh roses inside it, rearranging them to his liking. Once he'd done this, he took a step back and looked at the flowers.

He then looked over at Italia. "Whatchu think, babe?"

Italia smiled and gave him a thumb up. He smiled at her, pulled a chair up to her bed, and took her hand into his. He stared into her eyes. From the look on his face, she could tell something was troubling him. She just didn't know what it was, but she was sure he was about to tell her. At least, she hoped so for that matter.

"Since you've been laid up in here, I've hadda lotta time to think," Fear started, eyes becoming teary. "And I realize it's best that you and I don't continue to see one another. I live a dangerous and chaotic lifestyle. I know as long as you're in it, your life will always be hanging in the balance—waiting for one of my enemies to reach up and snatch it." Tears slid down his face unevenly, as he thought about one of his enemies snatching Italia's life away.

If he ever had to go on living without her, he wasn't sure if he'd make it or not. He was absolutely crazy about her. She was the air that he breathed. "That's why—that's why I gotta let chu go. I know my decision will hurt us both. But in the long run, I'd rather say goodbye now while you're still alive. Then to say it while I'm standing over your casket," he admitted, watching Italia's eyes fill with tears and spill out the corners of her eyes.

Fear took the time to wipe his dripping tears away with his curled finger. He then grasped Italia's hand with both of his and gently kissed it, lying it back down beside her. He bowed his head for a minute, and big teardrops fell from his eyes. He sniffled, wiped his eyes with the sleeve of his shirt, and rose to his feet, making his way out of Italia's room. As he reached her doorway, he glanced back at her and then continued through the door.

Chapter Fourteen

Once Lethal had been taken care of, a corrections officer escorted Gunplay down to segregation. As soon as Gunplay was in the hallway, he saw Two-Bit at the opposite end. Two-Bit was standing before another corrections officer with his wrists handcuffed behind his back. Both men smiled devilishly when they saw each other.

"So glad you could make it," Two-Bit said to Gunplay, as the corrections officer undid the handcuffs from around his wrists.

He'd paid the corrections officer to set up a fight between him and Gunplay. He was still heated about him getting in the way of him killing Lethal. Unfortunately, the day they'd engaged in their knife fight they'd been interrupted. Needless to say, Two-Bit was looking forward to wrapping up their unfinished business. Two-Bit was going to finish the job Lester had acquired his services for but he didn't want any further interference. He was sure he wouldn't have any once he'd gotten rid of Gunplay.

"I wouldn't miss it for the world," Gunplay replied, as the corrections officer undid the handcuffs from around his wrists. He took the shank the corrections officer passed him and watched as the other corrections officer passed Two-Bit one.

"I'm gonna cut off your ugly-ass face and wear it for Halloween," Two-Bit swore, as he and Gunplay circled one another, shanks up, ready to engage in mortal combat.

"I'd like to see you fucking try!" Gunplay retorted, with a feral snarl, he lunged forward and stabbed Two-Bit in the chest.

Two-Bit jumped back and touched his wound, fingertips coming away bloody. He sucked the blood off his fingers and spat it on the floor. He smiled psychopathically at him. "Now, the funs getting started—the first draw of blood is yours, but I'll be the only one leaving with a body!" Two-Bit's voice raised a few octaves, as he tried sticking Gunplay three times.

Gunplay swiftly avoided his attacks. He tried to counter, but Two-Bit kicked the hand that held his shank aside. Two-Bit then followed up, jabbing him in the chest twice, which caused

Gunplay to wince. He swung his shank trying to slash Two-Bit's throat, but he ducked his attempt. When Two-Bit came back up, he kicked him in the stomach. The blow doubled Gunplay over and left his face exposed. Two-Bit took advantage of his vulnerability and slashed him across the face.

"Gaaaaah!" Gunplay staggered backward and touched his face. He looked at his fingertips and they were bloody. This pissed him off. He really was about to get into Two-Bit's ass now. Screaming angrily, he charged at Two-Bit and Two-Bit did the same. Two-Bit and Gunplay exchanged pain-filled screams and stab wounds. Their blood dotted the floors and walls. The scenery became bloodier and bloodier until the corrections officers decided to break up the knife fight.

***

"Aaaaaah!" Gunplay hollered from his painful wounds, as he was rushed into the infirmary on a gurney. Two-Bit, hollering in pain also was rushed in on a gurney right behind him. They were both covered in blood and constantly bleeding. The medical staff was running back and forth across the infirmary floor, gathering everything they'd needed to start working on them. The entire facility was in an uproar, but things eventually calmed down once the young men had been stabilized. Still, they needed major surgery for the wounds they'd sustained, and a rare blood type that the infirmary didn't have in stock. The doctor had to call for Gunplay and Two-Bit an air ambulance. They needed to get to the hospital fast if they had any chance of survival. A helicopter was the right transportation to get them to the nearest hospital quickly enough.

Gunplay and Two-Bit were loaded inside of an air ambulance helicopter and flown across the city. They landed on the yellow helipad which was marked by an H. The propellers of the helicopter continuously chopped through the air, making that loud ass noise. There was a cop, two paramedics, and a pilot on board. The paramedics went to unload Gunplay first. When they grabbed ahold of his gurney, his eyes popped open and he rose up, bending at his waist. Scowling, he removed the transparent oxygen mask from his nose and mouth. Then, he pointed a handgun with a silencer on its barrel at one of the medics. The paramedics' eyes bulged, and they swallowed the lump of fear in their throat. They were taken completely off guard by Gunplay being strapped.

Seeing the paramedics at Gunplay's mercy, the cop eased his hand toward his holstered gun. He unbuckled its strap and was about to pull it until he felt something cold against his cheek. The cop's eyes darted to their corners and found Two-Bit behind a handgun with a silencer on it. He was still wearing his transparent oxygen mask over his nose and mouth. Two-Bit pulled the gun out of the cop's holster and whacked him across the skull with it, knocking him out cold.

Two-Bit leaned up front to the pilot. "You try any slick shit and I'ma splatter your thoughts against the inside of this windshield. Do you comprehend?" The terrified pilot nodded. "Good. Here's where we're going—" Two-Bit went on to fill the pilot in where he would be taking them. Afterward, he took the handcuff key from the cop, passed it to one of the paramedics, and ordered him to unlock it.

At the same time, Two-Bit shot the chain that bound him to the handcuffs off, severing it completely. At gunpoint, he ordered the paramedics to carry the unconscious cop out of the helicopter. They were then told to lie on their stomachs, interlock their fingers behind their heads, and count to one hundred.

"Do exactly as I say 'cause I'm gonna be counting right along wit' chu. If I see y'all asses get up from this rooftop before that count is up, me and my nigga gon' start busting at y'all from this choppa. Now, do we have an understanding?" Gunplay called out as loud as he could from beneath the loud ass helicopter's propeller.

The paramedics nodded their understanding and did like they were instructed. Sure enough, Two-Bit and Gunplay watched them from the helicopter as it rose into the air. They counted from where they were perched, watching the paramedics and the cop grow smaller and smaller until they became dots to them.

***

Two-Bit and Gunplay were leaning up against opposite walls inside the hallway. They were sweaty, breathing heavily, and their uniforms were covered in holes and bloodstains. They'd been in a knife fight for thirty minutes straight. The victorious one would walk away with the bounty on Lethal's head. Surprisingly, Two-Bit and Gunplay were evenly matched in combat. Their dedication, determination, and hearts were what drove them both.

"I've gotta—I've gotta give it to you. Uh, what's your name, bruh?" Gunplay asked as he panted out of breath.

"Two-Bit—everyone calls me Two—Two-Bit—" Two-Bit told him, as he panted out of breath.

"Well, Two-Bit—I've gotta salute cho' G. You're the hardest white boy—I've come across." Gunplay took the time to wipe his sweaty forehead and left a bloody streak behind.

"I've gotta admit, you're—you're—with the shits, too."

"You know, I could really use someone with your—talents— within my organization."

"Uh-uh, I'm Blood 'til I die, ain't nothing gon' ever change that."

"My nigga, I don't care about the color you are or the color of the flag you claiming," Gunplay assured him. "The only color I care about is green."

Two-Bit's forehead wrinkled confusingly. "So, what're you talking about, then?"

"I'm talking about busting the fuck up outta here and building my own empire," he told him. "I plan on running my own thang down in South Carolina. I've gotta plug that's gon' front me some bricks of coke and dope. All I need is some muscle—that's where you come in."

"Nah, fuck that! I'm not gonna be anyone's lapdog. If I come into what you've got popping, we're splitting everything fifty, fifty, straight down the middle. That's the only way I'm getting down,"

Two-Bit assured him. If Gunplay turned down his offer, he was willing to continue their fight to the death. The way he saw it, his future didn't look so bright with all the murders he was fighting anyway.

Gunplay tucked his shank and extended his bloody hand. "Deal?"

Two-Bit looked at Gunplay's hand for a while, allowing it to linger. He wondered if he was trying to set him up. Looking into his eyes he didn't see any deception in them, so he took a chance. He tucked his shank and shook Gunplay's bloody hand with his. Right then, they'd made a deal sealed in blood.

"I guess the bets off," the corrections officer with Gunplay said, pocketing his three-hundred dollars.

"Guess so," the corrections officer with Two-Bit agreed, pocketing his three-hundred dollars as well.

"Now, how the fuck are we gonna get outta here?" Two-Bit inquired, wiping the side of his sweaty face and leaving a bloody steak behind.

"I've been doing some thinking since we've been on lock-down. I came up with a way we can get up outta here and start our lives over from scratch. It will acquire us getting plastic surgery, but it will be well worth it getting a second chance at life. You feel me?" Two-Bit nodded understandingly. "Good. Now, here's what I have in mind—"

Gunplay went on to fill Two-Bit in on what he had planned for their escape. They were to engage in a staged knife fight that would leave them wounded to the point they'd need medical attention outside of the jail. They'd pay off the staff inside the infirmary to forge the documents so they'd be airlifted by helicopter.

Then, once they arrived at the hospital, they'd hijack the helicopter and fly to a secluded location. There they'd meet who Two-Bit wouldn't find out was Lester until later. Lester would take them to a disclosed location where a plastic surgeon would give them entirely different looks. From there they'd be transported to South Carolina, where they'd start their own operation.

"What about him?" Two-Bit nodded to the cell Lethal was lying asleep in.

Gunplay looked back at Lethal's cell and turned back around to Two-Bit. "The money we'll get for murking him, we'll divide right down the middle. Keep in mind, I have to hit these C.O.'s hands and a few of my partners, but whatever is left is ours to split."

Two-Bit nodded while massaging his chin, thinking everything he was told over. "Okay. I can rock with that." Gunplay's eyes suddenly rolled, and his knees buckled, but Two-Bit caught him. "You straight?" he asked with concern, forehead wrinkled.

"Yeah. I'm good." Gunplay told him. "I just need to get to the infirmary, I've lost a lil' too much blood."

"What's up?" The corrections officer with Gunplay asked as he and the other corrections officer approached.

"You need to get homeboy to the infirmary. He's lost too much blood," Two-Bit informed them.

***

It was dark out, but the glow of the moon shone. The chirps of grasshoppers in the yellow, tall, weeded grass was the only noise disturbing the silent night. Lester was leaned up against a Shell tank truck, sipping a Heineken and occasionally glancing at his watch. He was waiting for Gunplay and Two-Bit to arrive. He'd just finished his beer and cast it aside when he heard the sound of a whirring propeller in the sky. He looked up and saw the helicopter lowering to the ground. The rotational pull of the helicopter's propeller ruffled Lester's clothes and disturbed the debris on the ground.

"Mothafuckaz made it," Lester smirked.

Quickly, he pulled a ski-mask out of his jacket and pulled it down over his face, adjusting its eye holes. He'd donned the mask so that the pilot wouldn't be able to identify him. The helicopter landed before him and he was surprised to see two heads. A smile spread across his lips seeing a very familiar face. He watched as

Two-Bit told the pilot something in his ear while holding his silenced handgun to the back of his neck. He gathered that he'd told the pilot to kill the engine of the bird, because shortly the propeller stopped, and silence filled the air.

"Is that who I think it is?" Lester asked, drawing Two-Bit's attention. Holding a black pillowcase, he started in Gunplay and Two-Bit's direction.

Two-Bit was in the middle of cuffing the pilot's hands behind his back when he looked up and noticed Lester. Lester passed Gunplay a black pillowcase which he passed to Two-Bit. Two-Bit removed the headgear from the pilot's head and pulled the pillowcase down over his head.

"Unc, is that you?" Two-Bit said smiling, recognizing Lester's voice. Lester had a very distinguishable face and a voice like Samuel L. Jackson.

"Yeah, it's me, Two." Lester opened his arms to receive who he affectionately called his nephew.

Excited to see the old man, Two-Bit shoved the pilot over to Gunplay and approached Lester. Still holding his handgun, Two-Bit hugged Lester like you would a relative you hadn't seen a long time at a family reunion. They patted each other on the back and held one another at arm's length, looking each other over.

"Man, I had no idea I was springing yo' white ass from the joint. Good to see you, it's been a while, kid."

"Good to see you too, unc," Two-Bit told him. "You look great, man. You don't look a day over thirty."

"Aye, black doesn't crack." He chuckled.

"I'ma white boy, G. you know I wouldn't know nothing about that," Two-Bit replied. "I see you in shape. I may have to get in them gloves wit' chu and see if you still got it or not." He threw one-handed phantom punches at him while holding his handgun.

Lester bobbed, weaved, and threw a few phantom punches of his own. "Boy, it sure is good to see you, bring it in again." Lester opened his arms and Two-Bit hugged him again.

He then patted his adopted nephew on the shoulder and turned to Gunplay. Gunplay was forcing the pilot to lay on his stomach at gunpoint.

"Please, man, please, don't kill me!" the pilot pleaded for his life.

"Cuz shut cho' bitch-ass up!" Gunplay kicked the pilot in his side, and he grumbled in pain. "I already said I wasn't gon' splash yo' ol' scary-ass, so relax before I change my mind." A sharp whistle snatched Gunplay's attention from the pilot.

He looked over his shoulder and Two-Bit tossed him a copper-brown leather duffle bag. Lester was halfway inside the Mac truck. He grabbed a second identical duffle bag and tossed it over to Two-Bit.

"Fuck is this?" Gunplay's forehead wrinkled, wondering.

"A change of clothes and shoes," Lester informed him, "Unless you plan on walking around like that." He pointed at Gunplay's bloody jail uniform.

Gunplay looked down at his attire. He sat his handgun down inside the helicopter and stripped down to get dressed. Two-Bit was following suit. Once Gunplay and Two-Bit were dressed, Lester walked over to them with two oxygen masks attached to separate metal and green oxygen tanks. He handed each of them an oxygen mask and tank, explaining to them how they worked.

"Like I was saying, it's gonna take us a few hours to get where we're going, but you'll have more than enough oxygen in those tanks to tie you over," Lester assured them, with a hand on each of their shoulders. "If you gotta shit, I suggest you do that now. I have a couple of rolls of toilet paper in the truck." He looked between Gunplay and Two-Bit. They shook their heads, no. "Good. There's already a couple of five-gallon jugs in the truck if you've gotta piss. Plus, I packed y'all a few sandwiches and something to drink." He glanced at the timepiece on his wrist. "Okay, y'all, let's get a move on it."

Lester started walking over to his tanker truck, but the sound of his cellular ringing stopped him. He pulled it out of his pocket and answered the call, placing the cell phone to his ear.

"What's up?" Lester greeted the caller.

"Y'all straight?" Fear asked.

Lester looked over his shoulder at Gunplay and Two-Bit before answering, "Yeah, everything is copacetic, you good?"

"Yeah, I'm good. Yo, lemme holla at Gun, unc."

"Sure. Here he go." Lester passed the cell phone to Gunplay, telling him who it was on the cellular.

"What up, big bro?" Gunplay spoke into the cell phone.

"Ain't shit, just checking up on you," Fear told him. "You got them bandz I sent chu?"

Lester held open a duffle bag full of bankrolls secured by rubber-bands for Gunplay to see. He then zipped the bag back up. Gunplay gave him a thumb up, letting him know he'd seen the gwap. "Yeah, I got it, OG, showed me it. That's good looking out, my boy. I really appreciate it."

"Don't mention it," Fear responded. "Look, you know this will probably be the last time we hear from one another. You'll have to stay low-key and keep off the radar, even when you get the surgery. You can never be too careful. You know what I mean?"

"Yeah, I know. Once I touch down in the south, I'ma lay my hustle down and stack some major paypa up. Then, I'ma getting the fuck outta America. I'll probably take my black ass to the motherland, or to an island or some shit. Just experience a whole 'nother way of life. You know what I'm saying?" Gunplay looked up to Lester letting down the seats in the truck, which revealed a compartment large enough for a person to crawl into. The tank of the truck was completely empty, so Gunplay and Two-Bit had plenty of room to move around. Lester pushed a button that instantly opened the compartment. He motioned Two-Bit over once he'd looped the oxygen mask over his nose and mouth and he crawled inside the tank.

"I definitely feel where you're coming from. You know, you can hit me up if you need anything, right?"

"Yeah, I know. The same goes for me." Gunplay watched as Lester motioned for him to come on.

He held up a finger, signaling for him to give him one minute. Lester glanced at his timepiece and held up a thumb, which let him know he was good for the minute he'd asked for.

"I love you, lil' bruh, thanks for remaining solid when so many other niggaz would have folded."

"I love you too, big bruh. Peace."

"Peace." Fear disconnected the call.

Gunplay tossed the cellular to Lester and he stuck it inside his pocket. Gunplay put on the oxygen mask and picked up the tank. He climbed through the compartment and got comfortable inside the truck's tank. Lester shut the compartment and let the seats back. Pulling off his ski-mask, he tucked it into his back pocket and climbed into the truck. Once he shut the driver's door, he slapped on a trucker's cap, slipped a toothpick into his mouth, and cranked up the truck. Right after, he adjusted the side view mirror and pulled off.

Chapter Fifteen

Gunplay and Two-Bit's plastic surgery was a success. They were unrecognizable to those who knew them and to each other as well. This was exactly how they wanted it. They stayed an extra month at the location where the procedure was performed, so they could have their tattoos removed through laser surgery. They were given new identification cards, social security cards, birth certificates, passports among other things. They boarded a Delta Airlines flight to South Carolina, which took six hours from where they were holed up. It was six-thirty-five in the morning when their plane landed. They had a hard time haling a cab to Hertz car Rental Company, so they caught a shuttle bus there instead. They procured a big black van and set out to the part of town where Gunplay was to meet his plug.

Along the way, they stopped in the city of Irmo to pick up some guns from an arms dealer that Lester frequently conducted business with. Although Gunplay had had many conversations with his plug before flying out, he didn't know him that well. Old Boy, as he was called, was the cousin of one of his homeboys from his hood. Though Gunplay's comrade was a standup nigga, he didn't know how his people rocked. So, with an understanding that some wolves wore sheep's clothing, Gunplay wanted to be strapped to ensure he and Two-Bit's safety.

Lester, Gunplay, and Two-Bit's travels led them to the Colony Apartments formerly known as the George Washington Village Apartments. When Gunplay finally laid his eyes on Old Boy, he understood why he was given his nickname. He was twenty years old and had the face of a nigga in his sixties. It tripped Gunplay the fuck out. He didn't know if that disease Benjamin Button had was real, but if it was, he was sure Old Boy's ass had it. Old Boy was a five-foot-five, dark-skinned brother with slanted eyes, a wide nose, and big lips. He wore a nappy gold Mohawk and a white V-neck T-shirt, underneath a black leather vest.

The nigga was real hospitable and came off like he'd known

them for years. Still, no matter how cool homie was, Gunplay knew a gangsta when one was in his presence. It wasn't just his aura but the company he kept. The two goons chilling inside the kitchen with black Uzis by their sides confirmed for Gunplay that Old Boy was a young nigga that was serious about his business—all fun and games aside.

Old Boy was sitting down at the kitchen table with a fat ass blunt wedged between his fingers, pulling brick after brick out of a duffle bag. When he finished, he had a total of ten bricks on the table, stacked up and separated by five.

"A'ight," Old Boy began before blowing out a cloud of smoke. "Dat's five kilos of dope and five kilos of coke—like you requested." He took the time to suck on the end of his blunt and blew out a few clouds of smoke.

"Although I appreciate you blessing me with this package on consignment, I'd really like to test out the product, if that's okay wit' chu," Gunplay said, rubbing his hands together hopefully. He knew the drugs he was being given wasn't for free; he'd eventually have to pay for them. So, it was only right he knew what kind of merchandise he had on his hands.

"Okay. Cool." Old Boy nodded. "I can snag you a hype right quick."

"Yeah." Gunplay nodded. "I'd appreciate it, man."

Old Boy hollered at one of his goons, telling him to snatch up a dope fiend for them to test out the Boy. The goon returned ten-minutes later with a dope fiend of mixed descent. He was a six-foot-tall brother with curly, sandy-brown hair. He had a scruffy beard and awfully blemished skin. His attire was a raggedy, navy-blue blazer with one pocket hanging off it; a dirty wife-beater that looked like it was worn by Bruce Willis in Die Hard and fading black jeans five sizes too big. In fact, his jeans were so big he wore a rope to hold them bitchez up around his waist.

Old Boy blew out a cloud of smoke before making introductions. "My niggaz meet Charlie. Charlie meet my niggaz."

Lester, Gunplay, and Two-Bit gave the old dope fiend nods of acknowledgment.

"Yeah, yeah, yeah, where the dope y'all wanted me to sample?" Charlie looked around the apartment, licking his lips and rubbing his hands together greedily.

Old Boy chuckled and shook his head. He found it funny that the only thing that Charlie's ass cared about was getting high. But then again, what else should he expect from a dope fiend?

"Man, give dis nigga some of dat shit so he can shoot up." Old Boy motioned for one of his goons to fulfill the task. The goon did exactly what was asked of him. Charlie sat down at the kitchen table and prepared a syringe full of dope. He held it up and thumped it with his fingers, licking his lips thirstily. Everyone watched Charlie closely as he squirted some of the dope out of the tip of the needle. He sat the syringe down on the table and removed his blazer, hanging it on the back of his chair. Removing his blazer put his scrawny scab riddled arms on full display. Charlie went about his business, pulling the rope out of his jeans and then tying it around his forearm. Once he discovered a plump vein, he licked his thumb and rubbed it against it.

Charlie focused on his arm as he picked up the syringe, easing its needle inside his vein. He cracked a gummy smile and pushed down on the plunger, tainting his bloodline with the heroin. Once the drug had Charlie feeling euphoric, he threw his head back and shut his eyes. A smile curled his lips and he slumped down in his chair, rubbing on his dick in a sexual manner. His hand swung out to his side and left the syringe inside of the vein in his forearm. He turned his head from side to side moaning and smiling. Suddenly, Charlie winced and his eyes bulged.

His body went as limp as a cooked noodle and he fell out of his chair, crashing to the floor. He lay on his side with his jeans hanging around his thighs, exposing his shit-stained Fruit of the Loom briefs. Charlie's eyelids fluttered and flickered whiteness. His lips turned bluish-black and his heart thudded harder than usual. He started breathing erratically. Then, he made gurgling noises and foam oozed out of his mouth, dripping onto the floor. As Charlie's body was racked by convulsions, Gunplay and Two-Bit exchanged glances and focused their attention back on him.

After a while, Charlie's convulsions stopped, and he went still.

Old Boy snuffed out the ember of his blunt inside the ashtray and wisps of smoke rose into the air. He kneeled to Charlie and placed two fingers to the pulse in his neck. It was nonexistent. Old Boy looked to Gunplay and shook his head, letting him know that old Charlie was dead.

Gunplay and Two-Bit looked at one another smiling. They dapped up and gave each other a gangsta hug. Although dope fiend Charlie dying was a tragedy, it meant that Gunplay and Two-Bit had some supreme dope on their hands, and they were about to make a lot of money off it.

"Yeaaah, boy, niggaz 'bouta eat and eat good!" Gunplay dapped up with Lester as well.

He was happy for them so he was smiling. "We're gonna have to cut this shit with something, though. Mothafuckaz keep on dropping dead we're not gonna have any fiends to make money off."

Gunplay picked up the brick of dope from the table and examined it, smiling.

Yeah, me and my niggaz 'bout have these projects on smash! South Carolina get ready to meet the new King of the South!

***

Italia no longer being around allowed Fear and Constance to spend majority of their time together. They spent most of their time going on jobs and having sex—unprotected. Eventually, the latter caught up to them and Constance brought Fear news of her being pregnant. She was overly excited about the life growing inside her. Though Fear wasn't feeling fatherhood, he put up one hell of a front. He wasn't nearly as happy as Constance was about the baby. Constance thought he was though, but she was as wrong as two left sneakers.

Fear made no illusions of who he was and what he did for a living. There was no way he could raise a child given his lifestyle. Even if he turned his back on the game, he still had to worry about his past coming back to haunt him. His enemies could use the love of his child against him and have him in a fucked up situation. He didn't want to have to deal with that. He felt life would be much better without having to worry about taking care of a child. In his heart, he knew he was right, but it would be impossible to convince Constance to go through with an abortion. She had her heart set on welcoming a little boy or girl into the world. He was positive she would turn a deaf ear to whatever he had to say contrary to it.

One day tragedy struck while Constance was moving about in the kitchen fixing a bag of popcorn. The microwave dinged, and when she went to remove her snack an excruciating pain jolted through her stomach and southern region. She doubled over, blinking and wincing in pain, holding her stomach. The next thing she knew she was waking up on the floor in a small puddle of blood that was coming from between her legs.

She pulled herself up onto her feet, grabbed her car keys and jacket. She didn't bother to change her bloody clothes before she left the house; she wanted to get to the hospital as soon as possible to see if her baby was alright. Constance banged Fear's line on her way there. She and Fear reached Kaiser at the exact same time.

He walked her inside and they rushed her to the back. Constance and Fear discovered she'd had a miscarriage. She was devastated. She hollered to the Heavens asking God why he would bless her with such a precious gift and then rip it right out of her life.

"Oh, God, why? Why me Lord?" The tears flowed down her cheeks and she brought her hands to her face. She was lying in a hospital bed, in a sky-blue hospital gown with an IV hooked up to her arm. The doctor stood beside her rubbing her back and doing the best he could to comfort her. "What have I done?" she looked up at the ceiling. "What have I done to deserve this, Father? Haven't I been through enough? Haven't I been dealt enough pain in my life?" Her hands trembled uncontrollably and she looked at them as if they weren't part of her body. She breathed sporadically with her body twitching ever so often. She was hurt, broken, devastated, and overwhelmed.

"Get off me, don't chu fucking touch me!" She swung on the doctor and missed, but her next one connected, sending him sailing back.

He bumped into the neighboring bed, holding his jaw. She yanked the IV out of her hand and attacked him, throwing punches. He subdued her, wrapping his arms around her in a bear hug. She snuggled her face into his chest and sobbed her heart out. The nurse entered with a sedative, he motioned her in. He placed a finger to his lips telling her to be quiet. She crept in and gave Constance a shot. She went wild for a spurt, but eventually fell woozy and met with sleep. The doctor placed her in the bed and covered her up, turning off the light.

Hours later, Constance stirred awake. Her eyes were swollen from so much crying that it looked like she'd gotten into a fight. She looked beside her and found Fear lying asleep. A slight smirk formed on her lips seeing he'd stayed there the whole night with her.

"He stayed—he stayed the entire time," she spoke softly to no one in particular. She caressed the side of his head and kissed him on the temple.

Constance slid out of bed and made her way into the bathroom. Flipping on the light switch, she stepped before the sink and stared at her reflection in the mirror. She studied the altered version of herself. She couldn't help thinking about what her appearance and life had in common, they were both ugly. The thought fucked with her head. She found her shoulders shuddering and the tears rimming her eyes. She gripped both sides of the sink and bowed her head, her tears hit the sink and floor as she sobbed. The volume of her sobbing grew louder and louder.

"Shhhhhh," she heard him at her back, and when she looked up, he was wrapping his strong muscular arms around her.

Fear kissed her on the back of her head and nuzzled his nose in the nape of her neck. He placed two gentle kisses on her neck and looked at her reflection in the mirror.

"It's okay, it's alright," he whispered in her ear. "Everything is going to be just fine," he assured her.

She turned to him and her arms snaked around his body. She nestled the side of her face against his chiseled chest. "Hold me tight, Fear." He did like she'd asked. "Tighter, please."

Fear tightened his hold on her, pinning her against his warm body. He continued to whisper in her ear, slightly rocking her and rubbing her back. She didn't know what it was about his touch and his voice, but they made the perfect couple to soothe her pain in that moment.

"Tell me you love me," she said.

"Constance, I—"

"You don't have to mean it. I just need to hear you say it."

Fear closed his eyes as he took a deep breath. "I love you, Constance."

"Again."

"I love you, Constance."

Constance sobbed long and hard into Fear's white T-shirt, staining it with her tears and snot. Fear continued to comfort her with his gentle voice while rubbing her back. This was the first time he had ever shown that kind of affection to her. He didn't want to confuse her with what their relationship actually was, but seeing how she was breaking down, he had to step in and let her know he was there for her.

Constance decided to have a funeral for the baby she'd lost. Although she and Fear didn't know the sex, they both wanted it to be a boy, so they agreed to name him Nasir. They didn't have a body to bury so instead they put a memory in the ground. A beautiful burgundy wood stained coffin just big enough to fit a newborn was committed to the earth at Compton Cemetery. Surprisingly, Constance didn't shed a solitary tear that day. She lovingly kissed the casket and placed a long-stemmed rose upon it. She then treaded back toward the car on Fear's arm.

"I think I'm ready?" Constance told Fear, dabbing her wet eyes with his handkerchief.

Fear's face frowned and he said, "Ready for what?"

"To start my training."

"You sure? I mean, you don't wanna take the time to grieve after all of this?"

"No. It's best I lose myself in something, you know? Keep myself busy and my mind occupied."

Fear nodded understandingly and said, "Okay. Well, we'll set out tomorrow. How is that?"

"Cool." Constance dabbed her eyes some more, then slipped on her oversized shades to block out the sun. She interlocked her fingers with Fear, and they continued onto their whip.

Chapter Sixteen

The sky was partially cloudy, but the sun was shone, casting its light far and wide. There were insects moving about on trees and plants. There were also birds tweeting. One soared mid-level and glided passed Constance. Constance locs were pulled back in a ponytail, her face was free of makeup, and she was wearing a brown, hooded robe with a rope tied around her waist. She was submerged in the lakes water, which was really cold. A gathering of ducks sat on the surface of the water minding their own business, oblivious of Constance's presence, as she was theirs.

Fear appeared to be floating over the ground as he made his way toward the lake. He wore the hood of his black and white long sleeve clergy robe over his head, leaving the lower half of his face visible. Stitched on the back of his robe was League of Executioners. Below it there was a patch of a human skull with snakes coming out of its eye sockets and swords forming an X behind it. Below this patch was L.O. E the abbreviation for League of Executioners. Fear slowly descended into the lake making his way over to Constance. Once he was standing before her, he drew the hood back from his head, displaying six neat cornrows. He'd grown his hair out over the year he spent training Constance and had her braid his hair.

Fear took ahold of Constance's arm and placed his hand on top of her head. He advised her to shut her eyes, to which she did. Today was the day that the ceremony was taking place for her to be inducted into the League of Executioners. At that moment the baptism was taking place.

Fear gave a sermon that ended with, "Constance Payne Smith, I hereby baptize you in unholy water." He dunked his protégé into the water, quickly pulling her back up.

Drenched, Constance swiped the water out of her eyes and smiled at Fear. Excited about her rebirth, she rushed into Fear's arms, hugging, and kissing him affectionately. She pulled back and looked up into his eyes again, before hugging him once more.

The entire year in the mountains alone for Constance's training had brought her and Fear closer. They weren't exactly in a full-blown romantic relationship, but they had an understanding. They often had sex and leaned on one another for emotionally support, among other things. They were basically a couple, but without the title. Now, that's how Fear wanted it. Constance wanted more, but she knew her partner wouldn't budge, so she settled for what she could get.

Fear would go on to deal with several women. Desiree, Trishelle, Gloria, Chyna, Taraji, Unique, and a few others mysteriously vanished, thanks to Constance. Anyone who posed a threat to her position in Fear's life would get the business. She didn't give a fuck! If she couldn't have him then no one could. That's just how she felt.

Constance was surprised when Fear and Italia ended up reconnecting and falling in love all over again. The longer Italia's time got with him, the shorter Constance's time got with him, and she wasn't feeling that at all! What was worse was Fear had proposed to Italia again and was talking about giving up the murder for hire game. Him putting that out there caused Constance to wonder where that would leave her in his life. The thought of him going off and being happy with someone besides her made her sick. Again, she found herself in a position where she'd have to kill someone in order to keep *her* man. Although she knew the kind of heartache Italia's murder would bring Fear. She reasoned that it was a necessary evil and set out to handle her business.

Musiq Soulchild's Love played in the background as Italia moved around the room gracefully, setting the table for her and Fear's dinner that night. There was a roast with potatoes and carrots and homemade mashed potatoes smothered in gravy. To drink, she had an expensive bottle of white wine and for dessert, they were having blueberry cobbler. Once Italia had finished setting the table, she dimmed the lights and lit the vanilla-scented candles. She picked up a glass and poured a little white wine. When she sat the bottle of wine down and took a sip from her glass, the doorbell chimed.

"Oh, that's my baby!" Italia beamed brightly.

She headed toward the door, stopping to straighten herself up in the oval-shaped mirror along the way. She unlocked the door and pulled it open, smiling from ear to ear. The smile declined from her face once she discovered Constance standing before her. She looked over both of her shoulders and over her head, hoping to see Fear, but he wasn't anywhere in sight.

"Constance, what're you doing here?" She asked, displeased with her presence.

"Fear—I mean, Alvin, wanted you to know that he was going to be a little late and that he was sorry, so he sent me over with these." She presented her with a dozen long-stemmed red roses and that smile of hers made an encore.

Italia closed her eyes as she inhaled the scent of the roses, her smile expanding even wider. "Well, thanks, I'll throw these in some water." She went to close the door and Constance stuck her foot in, stopping the door from closing shut.

Italia looked down at the Timberland that blocked the path of the door and scrunched her face, looking back up at Constance irritated.

"You mind if I use your bathroom right quick?" Constance smirked.

Italia threw up a counterfeit smile and said, "Sure, why not?" She stepped aside, granting Constance entrance inside of her home. She took inventory of Constance's attire as she crossed the threshold and rolled her eyes. "You know, sweetie, there's no wonder why you never had a shot with Alvin. I mean, don't get me wrong. You're a pretty girl and all, but look at that nightmare you're wrapped up in. Black fatigues and Timberland boots. I swear, if I didn't know any better, I'd think there was cock and balls behind that zipper and not a vajayjay."

Constance stood with her back to Italia, looking around the living room. She rolled her eyes and mumbled something under her breath, agitated by the sound of Italia's voice. Her vocals were the equivalent of simmering, hot sewing needles being jabbed in and out of her eardrums over and over again. She wished she would just shut her fucking pie-hole.

"We're the only ones here?" she asked innocently.

"Girl, this is my place. I don't rock with roommates," Italia spat with attitude, one manicured hand on her hip as she rolled her neck. "The bathroom is down the hall and to your right." She motioned with a manicured finger. She then headed into the kitchen.

While her back was turned, Constance picked up the butcher's knife from the table where it laid beside the roast. Italia filled a clear, see-through, glass vase with water and dropped the long-stemmed roses into it, spreading them out. She inhaled the fresh, sweet scent of the roses and picked up the vase, smiling. She'd just turned around when something sharp slammed through her chest, hitting bone. Her eyes looked like they were about to pop out of their sockets and her mouth shot open. She croaked and released the vase, it exploded when it hit the floor, sending broken shards flying everywhere.

Italia looked down at the butcher's knife buried into her chest down to the handle. Her thick blood traveled the length of the blade and dripped onto the floor. Red droplets splattered as they hit her Manolo Blahnik high heel pumps. Her white, Narciso Rodriguez, low-high gown quickly soaked up the blood like a maxi pad.

Italia looked up from the handle and into the malicious orbs that were Constance's pupils. She tried to say something, but the pain in her chest paralyzed her vocal cords.

Constance placed a finger to her lips. Keeping eye contact with her she said, "Shhh, I want you to understand something, he belongs to me. He's mine." She pushed the knife upward, lifting Italia to the tips of her Manolo's. "And he always will be. I'm not gon'—" Italia tried to say something again, but only succeeded in coughing up blood. Constance hushed her and said, "No, listen. I'm not gon' let you or 'nan other bitch take him away from me, okay? Before I let that happen, I'll kill you and a hunnit more hoes that look just like you."

A devilish smile curled Constance's lips as she combed her gloved hand through Italia's long expensive weave, watching the tears pool in her eyes and spill down her cheeks. Blood flooded Italia's grill and spilled down her chin, dripping on the floor. Constance broke the knife off in her chest bone and shoved her back, causing her to fall up against the wall. She then dropped the other half of the knife and sat down at the table. She stuffed a napkin cloth into her shirt and prepared herself a plate.

Eating, she watched Italia attentively. Her eyes became lazy and she struggled for breath. Her white gown was covered in so much blood that you would have thought she'd purchased it in that color. Once Italia's body went slack and she unleashed her last breath, Constance ate, washed her dishes, and left.

***

Fifteen Minutes Later

Fear was fitted in a sweater vest and plaid shirt when he finally arrived at Italia's house. He was smiling from ear to ear, looking good and smelling even better. He adjusted his collar and switched hands with the bouquet of roses he'd brought, knocking on the front door. Clearing his throat, he surveyed his surrounding like he always had. He was in a profession that made him a hell of a lot of enemies.

So, it was best he stayed strapped and paid close attention to his surroundings, to avoid getting caught slipping. Fear knocked on the door louder this time since no one had answered beforehand. Three minutes later, finding it odd no one had come to the door, he decided to try the doorknob. To his surprise, the doorknob clicked as he twisted it and he made his way inside. As soon as he saw Italia lying on the floor in a pool of her own blood, his heart shattered like glass, raining down in a million little pieces. His eyes quickly collected water and spilled down his cheeks. He released the bouquet of roses and they deflected off his right foot, landing on the floor. His mouth hung open and his bottom lip quivered uncontrollably.

"My baby, nah, baby no, no, no, no—" Fear made an ugly face as he wept, coating his cheeks layers and layers of tears. He dropped down to his hands and knees, crawling over to Italia. "Don't leave me, don't leave me, baby. You can't, you can't leave me all alone," he told Italia as he held her in his arms, rocking back and forth. Big teardrops fell from the brims of his eyes and transparent snot oozed out of his nose. "Awwww, I need you, baby. I need you, no! No, no, no, no! Come back, please, come back!" He threw his head back looking up at the ceiling talking to God. He had tears and snot rolling over his lips, sliding down his chin. "Don't chu do it! You hear me? Don't chu dare do it! Give her back, give her back to me! God damn you! You hear me? Goddamn youuuuuu!" Suddenly, Fear bowed his head and kissed Italia's lips tenderly, sweeping her eyes shut.

He stayed with her for three hours before calling 9-1-1. As soon as he hung up from talking with the emergency dispatcher, he hit up Constance and told her what happened. His voice was shaky with emotion when he was talking with her. He was distraught and shaken, and she could tell he was trying his best not to break down crying.

Constance told Fear she was on her way over, hopping into her whip and speeding to his location. When she arrived at Italia's house, the front was lit up by the blue and red lights of police cars. There was also a coroner van parked out front, and two men were loading a body inside it. In front of the van, there was an unmarked Crown Victoria, which Constance assumed was driven by the detective that came out to investigate the homicide.

Constance hopped out of her car and slammed the door shut behind her, dashing toward Italia's crib. When she made her way inside, she found Fear leaning in the doorway of the kitchen. He was talking to a detective who was writing down everything he was being told. Although Fear wasn't crying, she could tell by his pink, glassy eyes that he had been at some point.

Once the detective finished his questioning, he patted him on his shoulder and walked away. At that time, Constance locked eyes with Fear, sensing the hurt he was experiencing without him uttering a word. She took off running toward him. They collided in an affectionate embrace. He melted in her arms, body shaking, as he looked over her shoulder. Tears poured down his cheeks and he bit down on his bottom lip, stifling his cries. He was very prideful and didn't want her to hear him sobbing. He didn't want to taint the image of him that she had.

"Stop it! You hear me? Stop that shit, right now," Constance said seriously, wearing a stern expression. "You don't have to be strong all of the time, baby. You can be vulnerable with me. I accept you. I accept you wholeheartedly." She kissed him on the side of his neck. That kiss and those words broke him down. A wave of emotions swept through Fear's body and he sobbed long and hard, trembling awfully. The tears flowed and flowed, drenching his face. Constance tightened her embrace and kissed him again. "That's it. Let it all out, let it all out," she encouraged him, and he continued to grieve. "It's just you and I now, baby. You hear me?"

"Ye—yes," Fear's voice cracked with raw emotion.

"Uh-uh, I need to hear it. Lemme hear you say it, baby."

"It's just—it's just you—and—and I."

"That's right. And don't chu ever forget that," Constance told him. "I'll never let anyone take you away from me—ever." She looked over his shoulder at her reflection in the oval-shaped mirror on the wall. Her face reddened and black horns curved out of either side of her forehead. Her eyes turned into those of a cat and a smile spread across her face, showcasing fangs.

THE END

Submission Guideline

Submit the first three chapters of your completed manuscript to ldpsubmissions@gmail.com, subject line: Your book's title. The manuscript must be in a .doc file and sent as an attachment. Document should be in Times New Roman, double spaced and in size 12 font. Also, provide your synopsis and full contact information. If sending multiple submissions, they must each be in a separate email.

Have a story but no way to send it electronically? You can still submit to LDP/Ca$h Presents. Send in the first three chapters, written or typed, of your completed manuscript to:

LDP: Submissions Dept
Po Box 944
Stockbridge, Ga 30281

DO NOT send original manuscript. Must be a duplicate.

Provide your synopsis and a cover letter containing your full contact information.

Thanks for considering LDP and Ca$h Presents.

Coming Soon from Lock Down Publications/Ca$h Presents

BOW DOWN TO MY GANGSTA

By **Ca$h**

TORN BETWEEN TWO

By **Coffee**

THE STREETS STAINED MY SOUL **II**

By **Marcellus Allen**

BLOOD OF A BOSS **VI**

SHADOWS OF THE GAME II

By **Askari**

LOYAL TO THE GAME **IV**

By **T.J. & Jelissa**

A DOPEBOY'S PRAYER **II**

By **Eddie "Wolf" Lee**

IF LOVING YOU IS WRONG… **III**

By **Jelissa**

TRUE SAVAGE **VII**

MIDNIGHT CARTEL III

DOPE BOY MAGIC IV

CITY OF KINGZ II

By **Chris Green**

BLAST FOR ME **III**

A SAVAGE DOPEBOY III

CUTTHROAT MAFIA III

By **Ghost**

A HUSTLER'S DECEIT III

KILL ZONE **II**

BAE BELONGS TO ME III

A DOPE BOY'S QUEEN II

By **Aryanna**

COKE KINGS V

KING OF THE TRAP II

By **T.J. Edwards**

GORILLAZ IN THE BAY V

De'Kari

THE STREETS ARE CALLING II

Duquie Wilson

KINGPIN KILLAZ IV

STREET KINGS III

PAID IN BLOOD III

CARTEL KILLAZ IV

DOPE GODS III

Hood Rich

SINS OF A HUSTLA II

ASAD

KINGZ OF THE GAME V

Playa Ray

SLAUGHTER GANG IV

RUTHLESS HEART IV

By **Willie Slaughter**

THE HEART OF A SAVAGE III

By **Jibril Williams**

FUK SHYT II

By **Blakk Diamond**

THE REALEST KILLAZ II

By **Tranay Adams**

TRAP GOD II

By **Troublesome**

YAYO IV

A SHOOTER'S AMBITION III

By S. Allen

GHOST MOB

Stilloan Robinson

KINGPIN DREAMS III

By Paper Boi Rari

CREAM

By Yolanda Moore

SON OF A DOPE FIEND III

By Renta

FOREVER GANGSTA II

GLOCKS ON SATIN SHEETS III

By Adrian Dulan

LOYALTY AIN'T PROMISED II

By Keith Williams

THE PRICE YOU PAY FOR LOVE II

DOPE GIRL MAGIC III

By Destiny Skai

CONFESSIONS OF A GANGSTA II

By Nicholas Lock

I'M NOTHING WITHOUT HIS LOVE II

By Monet Dragun

LIFE OF A SAVAGE IV

A GANGSTA'S QUR'AN II

MURDA SEASON II

By **Romell Tukes**

QUIET MONEY III

THUG LIFE II

By **Trai'Quan**

THE STREETS MADE ME III

By **Larry D. Wright**
THE ULTIMATE SACRIFICE VI
IF YOU CROSS ME ONCE II
ANGEL III
By **Anthony Fields**
THE LIFE OF A HOOD STAR
By **Ca$h & Rashia Wilson**
FRIEND OR FOE II
By **Mimi**
SAVAGE STORMS II
By **Meesha**
BLOOD ON THE MONEY II
By **J-Blunt**

Available Now

RESTRAINING ORDER **I & II**
By **CA$H & Coffee**
LOVE KNOWS NO BOUNDARIES **I II & III**
By **Coffee**
RAISED AS A GOON I, II, III & IV
BRED BY THE SLUMS I, II, III
BLAST FOR ME I & II
ROTTEN TO THE CORE I II III
A BRONX TALE I, II, III
DUFFEL BAG CARTEL I II III IV

HEARTLESS GOON I II III IV

A SAVAGE DOPEBOY I II

HEARTLESS GOON I II III

DRUG LORDS I II III

CUTTHROAT MAFIA I II

By **Ghost**

LAY IT DOWN **I & II**

LAST OF A DYING BREED

BLOOD STAINS OF A SHOTTA I & II III

By **Jamaica**

LOYAL TO THE GAME I II III

LIFE OF SIN I, II III

By **TJ & Jelissa**

BLOODY COMMAS I & II

SKI MASK CARTEL I II & III

KING OF NEW YORK I II,III IV V

RISE TO POWER I II III

COKE KINGS I II III IV

BORN HEARTLESS I II III IV

KING OF THE TRAP

By **T.J. Edwards**

IF LOVING HIM IS WRONG...I & II

LOVE ME EVEN WHEN IT HURTS I II III

By **Jelissa**

WHEN THE STREETS CLAP BACK I & II III

THE HEART OF A SAVAGE I II

By **Jibril Williams**

A DISTINGUISHED THUG STOLE MY HEART I II & III

LOVE SHOULDN'T HURT I II III IV

RENEGADE BOYS I II III IV

Tranay Adams

PAID IN KARMA I II III

SAVAGE STORMS

By **Meesha**

A GANGSTER'S CODE I &, II III

A GANGSTER'S SYN I II III

THE SAVAGE LIFE I II III

CHAINED TO THE STREETS I II III

BLOOD ON THE MONEY

By J-Blunt

PUSH IT TO THE LIMIT

By **Bre' Hayes**

BLOOD OF A BOSS **I, II, III, IV, V**

SHADOWS OF THE GAME

By **Askari**

THE STREETS BLEED MURDER **I, II & III**

THE HEART OF A GANGSTA I II& III

By **Jerry Jackson**

CUM FOR ME I II III IV V

An **LDP Erotica Collaboration**

BRIDE OF A HUSTLA **I II & II**

THE FETTI GIRLS **I, II& III**

CORRUPTED BY A GANGSTA I, II III, IV

BLINDED BY HIS LOVE

THE PRICE YOU PAY FOR LOVE

DOPE GIRL MAGIC I II

By **Destiny Skai**

WHEN A GOOD GIRL GOES BAD

By **Adrienne**

THE COST OF LOYALTY I II III

By Kweli

A GANGSTER'S REVENGE **I II III & IV**

THE BOSS MAN'S DAUGHTERS I II III IV V

A SAVAGE LOVE **I & II**

BAE BELONGS TO ME I II

A HUSTLER'S DECEIT I, II, III

WHAT BAD BITCHES DO I, II, III

SOUL OF A MONSTER I II III

KILL ZONE

A DOPE BOY'S QUEEN

By **Aryanna**

A KINGPIN'S AMBITON

A KINGPIN'S AMBITION **II**

I MURDER FOR THE DOUGH

By **Ambitious**

TRUE SAVAGE I II III IV V VI

DOPE BOY MAGIC I, II, III

MIDNIGHT CARTEL I II

CITY OF KINGZ

By **Chris Green**

A DOPEBOY'S PRAYER

By **Eddie "Wolf" Lee**

THE KING CARTEL **I, II & III**

By **Frank Gresham**

THESE NIGGAS AIN'T LOYAL **I, II & III**

By **Nikki Tee**

GANGSTA SHYT **I II &III**

By **CATO**

THE ULTIMATE BETRAYAL

By **Phoenix**

BOSS'N UP **I , II & III**

Tranay Adams

By **Royal Nicole**
I LOVE YOU TO DEATH
By Destiny J
I RIDE FOR MY HITTA
I STILL RIDE FOR MY HITTA
By **Misty Holt**
LOVE & CHASIN' PAPER
By **Qay Crockett**
TO DIE IN VAIN
SINS OF A HUSTLA
By **ASAD**
BROOKLYN HUSTLAZ
By **Boogsy Morina**
BROOKLYN ON LOCK I & II
By **Sonovia**
GANGSTA CITY
By **Teddy Duke**
A DRUG KING AND HIS DIAMOND I & II III
A DOPEMAN'S RICHES
HER MAN, MINE'S TOO I, II
CASH MONEY HO'S
By Nicole Goosby
TRAPHOUSE KING **I II & III**
KINGPIN KILLAZ I II III
STREET KINGS I II
PAID IN BLOOD **I II**
CARTEL KILLAZ I II III
DOPE GODS I II
By **Hood Rich**
LIPSTICK KILLAH **I, II, III**

CRIME OF PASSION I II & III

FRIEND OR FOE

By **Mimi**

STEADY MOBBN' **I, II, III**

THE STREETS STAINED MY SOUL

By **Marcellus Allen**

WHO SHOT YA **I, II, III**

SON OF A DOPE FIEND I II

Renta

GORILLAZ IN THE BAY **I II III IV**

TEARS OF A GANGSTA I II

DE'KARI

TRIGGADALE I II III

Elijah R. Freeman

GOD BLESS THE TRAPPERS I, II, III

THESE SCANDALOUS STREETS I, II, III

FEAR MY GANGSTA I, II, III IV, V

THESE STREETS DON'T LOVE NOBODY I, II

BURY ME A G I, II, III, IV, V

A GANGSTA'S EMPIRE I, II, III, IV

THE DOPEMAN'S BODYGAURD I II

THE REALEST KILLAZ

Tranay Adams

THE STREETS ARE CALLING

Duquie Wilson

MARRIED TO A BOSS… I II III

By Destiny Skai & Chris Green

KINGZ OF THE GAME I II III IV

Playa Ray

SLAUGHTER GANG I II III

Tranay Adams

RUTHLESS HEART I II III

By Willie Slaughter

FUK SHYT

By Blakk Diamond

DON'T F#CK WITH MY HEART I II

By Linnea

ADDICTED TO THE DRAMA I II III

By Jamila

YAYO I II III

A SHOOTER'S AMBITION I II

By S. Allen

TRAP GOD

By Troublesome

FOREVER GANGSTA

GLOCKS ON SATIN SHEETS I II

By Adrian Dulan

TOE TAGZ I II III

By Ah'Million

KINGPIN DREAMS I II

By Paper Boi Rari

CONFESSIONS OF A GANGSTA

By Nicholas Lock

I'M NOTHING WITHOUT HIS LOVE

By Monet Dragun

CAUGHT UP IN THE LIFE I II III

By Robert Baptiste

NEW TO THE GAME I II III

By **Malik D. Rice**

LIFE OF A SAVAGE I II III

A GANGSTA'S QUR'AN

MURDA SEASON

By **Romell Tukes**

LOYALTY AIN'T PROMISED

By Keith Williams

QUIET MONEY I II

THUG LIFE

By **Trai'Quan**

THE STREETS MADE ME I II

By **Larry D. Wright**

THE ULTIMATE SACRIFICE I, II, III, IV, V

KHADIFI

IF YOU CROSS ME ONCE

ANGEL I II

By **Anthony Fields**

THE LIFE OF A HOOD STAR

By Ca$h & Rashia Wilson

Tranay Adams

BOOKS BY LDP'S CEO, CA$H

TRUST IN NO MAN
TRUST IN NO MAN 2
TRUST IN NO MAN 3
BONDED BY BLOOD
SHORTY GOT A THUG
THUGS CRY
THUGS CRY 2
THUGS CRY 3
TRUST NO BITCH
TRUST NO BITCH 2
TRUST NO BITCH 3
TIL MY CASKET DROPS
RESTRAINING ORDER
RESTRAINING ORDER 2
IN LOVE WITH A CONVICT
LIFE OF A HOOD STAR

Coming Soon
BONDED BY BLOOD 2
BOW DOWN TO MY GANGSTA